Reborn as Bree

THE SHADOWDANCE CLUB 5

AVERY GALE®

REBORN AS BREE
Copyright © 2013 by Avery Gale
ISBN: 978-1-944472-61-0
Print Edition

ALL RIGHTS RESERVED: This literary work may not be reproduced or transmitted in any form or by any means, including electronic or photographic reproduction, in whole or in part, without express written permission.

All characters and events in this book are fictitious. Any resemblance to actual persons living or dead is strictly coincidental.

Chapter 1

One Year Ago

JAMIE CREED ALWAYS agreed with his teammates when they had likened his role on their Special Forces team to a quote by the Joker in the movie *Batman*... *Do you ever dance with the devil in the pale moonlight?* It really was an apt description of how he spent a vast amount of his mission time. As one of the two snipers on the team, he usually found himself high above the real action. He was often relegated to watching everything unfold in the darkness below through a night vision scope that turned the entire world ominous shades of green and black.

His dance with the devil was always two-fold. First, he ended the lives of enemies, people whose absence helped mankind, but that didn't mean those actions didn't come at a cost—a very steep cost. The largest consequence was his karma debt, and he was afraid that was going to be more than he'd be able to clean from his slate in the next several lifetimes.

His *grand-mère* had always stressed to him that "a soul is a soul, and they are not ours to judge or take." His mother's mother was a Cajun priestess. She'd been a healer and prophet her entire life. *Grand-mère* was both revered and feared around his small bayou home. She had never seemed to spend much time with his numerous brothers and sisters or any other member of their enormous, extended family. Some of the family was scattered to the far corners of the world but most had remained fairly close to their bayou home. For some reason she'd never been willing to share, *Grand-mère* had always taken a particularly keen interest in Jamie.

He remembered sitting on the back step of her small shanty late at night, listening as she told him stories about his ancestors and all the ways *juju* had influenced the fates of various family members. She'd explained the power of destiny and tried to explain that he'd have many opportunities to make what she called *heart choices* and encouraged him to follow his *internal light*.

Jamie hadn't understood the power of her words until his first mission as a SEAL sniper. He had been lying on the roof of a building in temperatures so sweltering, he'd been sure the tar was going to glue him to the damned surface permanently. He'd managed to stay motionless for nearly thirteen hours when his target finally emerged from his home. Jamie's objective had been simple—eliminate the man and then disappear—but just as he'd pulled in his breath and was releasing it slowly and pulling back the trigger, the man turned, and Jamie noticed his target's hands.

The disguise had been flawless, except for the hands. The bastard had dressed a young woman in his clothing and sent her out the door first. Had Jamie not listened to that inner voice, he'd have killed an innocent, and the man who was selling weapons to any terrorist with the cash would have escaped once again. Jamie had always considered that his defining moment as a SEAL... at least until he'd been a last-minute add-on to a rescue mission.

Thinking back over all the life-altering and life-ending moments Jamie Creed had given others, it mystified him that the most significant one in his life hadn't occurred behind the anonymity of a long-range rifle shot. His own had come as he carried a battered waif from a rattan hut on the fringes of the Congo.

While he'd been running from the rat-infested hole where they'd found the young woman chained to hooks set in concrete, he'd looked down at the badly swollen face of Sabrina Gillette and wondered how many bones her captors had broken while beating her. How the hell she'd managed to survive the horrors they'd inflicted upon her?

There wasn't a single place he could see where she wasn't bloodied or bruised. He'd hated scooping her up so hurriedly, but the whole team was racing the clock, and he certainly wasn't going to risk her being recaptured by the madmen who'd imprisoned her.

He'd known the instant she'd realized she was no longer lying on that filthy floor but was, in fact, being cradled in the arms of a man she didn't recognize because her body had responded with a primal surge of fight-or-flight fear that had almost been palpable. But when she had fleetingly opened her eyes, he'd smiled and whispered, "It's alright, *Chère*, you're safe. I'm taking you home."

At his words, she had let her eyes drift closed but not before he'd seen the gratitude clearly written in them. He'd been haunted by those misty gray eyes ever since. Jamie had been relieved when she'd slipped back into unconsciousness because he was certain even though he was running as smoothly as possible, the jarring movements had to be creating excruciating pain for his precious cargo.

Looking down at her as he'd laid her on the pallet inside their "evac-chopper," he was stunned by the fact, that despite the damage her captors had done, she was still an ethereal beauty. Her long hair appeared to be blonde beneath the caked-on dirt and filth, and he'd wished she would open her eyes just once more, so he could memorize their color. But she hadn't, and he'd been forced to rely on his memories of that sweet moment. Since that afternoon, he'd seen the color a thousand times—in the softly falling mist of a rolling fog, the swirling depths of the Atlantic Ocean, and painting the feathers of a dove—but he'd never seen another person with eyes that shade of gray. That was the only time he'd even spoken to her, but he'd always been grateful she had realized he wasn't going to harm her and her expression had changed from fear to trust and relief.

It had been those brief moments that had changed the course of Jamie Creed's path in life. He'd been due to sign the paperwork to extend his service in the Special Forces when he returned stateside a few months later. Instead, he'd made a phone call to his former team leaders. Jamie accepted the job offer Alex and Zach Lamont had extended numerous times during the last two years of Creed's military service. Ending his military service had been the smartest decision he'd ever made.

Jamie's friend and fellow sniper, Ethan Jantz followed his lead and while Jamie had spent a month with his family in the bayou, Ethan had visited his family in Houston. Jamie had always laughed at the disparity in their backgrounds. His family had always been poor but hardworking and honest while Ethan's family was ungodly rich but from what Jamie could tell, they rarely worked. How Ethan's family maintained their wealth when they appeared to be as lazy as slugs and about as loyal as swamp snakes with the personalities of pissed-off gators was a mystery indeed.

With their obligatory visits home completed, they'd met up and traveled to Colorado together.

Working for the Lamonts as contract black-ops operators was much more rewarding, both personally and financially. Even though the money was a great perk, Jamie knew the allure of the work was doing something more altruistic, and he never turned down a job that involved the rescue of a hostage. He'd thought about Sabrina Gillette many times since her rescue, and when he'd finally been brave enough to Google her name, he'd been devastated to learn she hadn't survived her ordeal. Thankfully, the press hadn't printed any of the more gruesome details of her captivity. Jamie was sure her family had suffered enough without letting the entire world know their daughter had died because of their chosen line of work.

Chapter 2

Present Day

THE RAIN ENDED as quickly as it started. The weather in Colorado had always fascinated Creed. Being from the bayou, he was well accustomed to rain that came in torrents or as a slow-soaking mist that could stick around for days on end. After accepting an offer to join the crack team of operatives his former teammates had assembled, he had grown familiar with the sudden cloudbursts that seemed to race over the mountain peaks to raise holy hell for a few minutes to an hour, then disappear as quickly as they had arrived.

Visitors to The ShadowDance Club often commented on the inconsistency of the weather in Kansas, and he'd thought to himself if it was worse than Colorado, he was going to take a pass on "The Land of Oz." He did enjoy trying to calculate the amount of time it was going to take a rainstorm to race over the mountains, but then, he and his teammates were usually happy to bet on just about anything.

Moving through the trees rather than using the road was more out of habit than from necessity and having just returned from a particularly brutal mission in a jungle sauna on the other side of the globe, he was enjoying the cooler temperatures. The milder climate made the extra time it would take to make his way back to The Club more of a blessing than a hardship.

He loved the smell of the mountains and spent as much time outside learning every little secret there was to know about the area around the Lamonts' ShadowDance Mountain estate. Alex and Zach had grown up on the mountain, so they had been great sources of information in the beginning, but it was teammate Cash Red Cloud who had shown Jamie all the small caves and hiding places where he could stash weapons.

Cash's Native American heritage was as colorful as the meadows filled with wildflowers. The Red Cloud's family tree was full of warriors, so Cash understood better than anyone Jamie's need to always have a weapon nearby. The two of them had spent many hours uncovering the secrets the ShadowDance Mountain seemed to guard so fiercely.

Jamie stopped suddenly when he heard the sound of a car coming up the long winding drive. Looking through the sodden branches of the pines that lined the driveway, he watched as a young woman drove carefully up the road. Her eyes were glued to the blacktop, and Jamie wondered for a moment if she might not have run over him if he'd been walking along the side of the road.

Sprinting the last one hundred yards to the mansion, he was in place and well hidden by the time she pulled to a stop at the bottom of the wide staircase leading to The ShadowDance Club. It was Monday, so The Club wouldn't be opening until the next afternoon, and that information was clearly stated on the sign at the end of the drive, so he watched and waited to see exactly what she was up to. She just sat in her car for so long, he was just getting ready to tap his ear mike and ask his partner in the Crow's Nest if he had an ID on the women yet when she finally opened her car door.

BREE SAT IN her small car and stared at the beautiful building looming over her, wondering if perhaps her information had been wrong or she was lost... *again*. Was it really possible one of the most well respected BDSM clubs in the country was housed in such a picturesque location? And it looked like there was another even larger structure extending off from the one she was facing. *Holy shit, how big is this club, anyway? I know Mrs. Lamont said her sons had built a successful club but damn!*

Bree had met Catherine Lamont a few months ago when she'd volunteered at a rape crisis and domestic violence prevention center in Denver. Having moved back to the United States after living and working in the Congo for the past five years, Bree had seen a lot of violence directed at women and had experienced it firsthand a year earlier. She'd followed her missionary parents all over the world during a childhood that was anything but dull. After spending her college years stateside, she'd chosen to return to one of the most troubled spots in the world because she'd known just how valuable her medical training would be to the war-ravaged nations of central Africa.

She hadn't found out until after her kidnapping that missionary work had merely been a cover for her parents and nothing she'd thought she knew about her family had been the truth. She still struggled to accept the fact John and Christina Gillette had both been well-trained operators, and their frequent trips for "supplies" were actually highly orchestrated missions.

While recovering, she'd been faced with indisputable evidence, but something had never rung entirely true about the story. While a part of her had been relieved to discover the hatred the terrorists had displayed toward her hadn't been personal, it had been devastating to learn she was being forced to walk away from the work she had dedicated her life to. After her rescue, Sabrina Gillette had died, and Bree Hart had been born. Shaking off the dark memories threatening to bubble up and swamp her, Bree got out of the small car but didn't move up the stairs. Instead, she chose to sit at the bottom and just take in the spectacular view.

JAMIE SAT IN the shadows and watched as the stunning woman slowly got out of the tiny car and moved toward the steps. He'd expected her to go up the steps, and he'd started to give the inside watchman a heads-up when he noticed her turn and sit down on the bottom step, looking out over the fountains and hedges. She seemed content to just take in the beauty surrounding her, and he found himself taking a good look at the landscaping for the first time in the year he had been living here. Watching her closely, he wondered what was going through her thoughts. Double-checking his rifle to be sure it was clear, he raised the weapon, so he could use the high-power scope to get an up close and personal look at her.

He couldn't take his eyes off her. She was absolutely stunning. Her hair was the color of sun-ripened wheat and fell to her waist in gentle waves. Her skin looked like it was flawless ivory, and he'd bet his last nickel her eyes were blue and wasn't that going to be disappointing. He was forever going to be haunted by the misty gray eyes of Sabrina Gillette. Trying to follow her line of sight, he was surprised to see she wasn't looking at anything in particular, simply appeared to be enjoying the beauty surrounding her.

When it looked like she tensed, he lowered his scope. The woman obviously had good instincts because she'd apparently sensed someone watching her. He didn't want to spook her, so he moved quickly to a small alcove at the side of the building and secured his gear before sauntering around the side of The ShadowDance Club.

Jamie's plan was to be clearly in her line of sight long before he was close enough to speak to her. She would have plenty of time to see him before he got near her, ensuring she wouldn't be startled by his presence. His years of Special Forces recon training and experience could have gotten him close enough to touch her before she would have even known anyone was within a mile of her, but he'd seen the tension race through her and the telltale stiffening of her spine when she'd felt his gaze. He could think of a thousand and one things he'd like to do to her, but scaring her wasn't even on the list.

BREE SAW THE tall man with shaggy, jet-black hair moving toward her the minute he came around the corner of the building. Watching him walk with a catlike grace, she couldn't help but notice how smooth and unhurried his movements were. Every muscle was using the minimum amount of energy to generate the maximum results like a dancer or a predator. Shaking off the images *that* brought to mind, she refocused on projecting a professional persona and was doing fine until she looked up into his eyes.

As he'd gotten close enough for her to look into his eyes, she'd been overwhelmed by the feeling she'd just taken a refreshing dive into the Caribbean Sea. He had the most amazingly cerulean eyes she'd ever seen. They were the clearest azure blue imaginable. She just stared at him for what seemed like hours but couldn't have been more than a few seconds. Bree saw his mouth moving but couldn't hear past the roar of the blood rushing in her ears.

How am I supposed to have an intelligent conversation with someone when I'm lost in their eyes? Damn, get it together, or he's going to think you're an idiot!

Chapter 3

BREE SUDDENLY REALIZED she was sitting on a leather sofa in front of a beautiful stone fireplace. The fire danced with abandon beneath a hearth that looked like a solid piece of granite. *I wonder how heavy that is? Who on earth can afford to buy that, much less move it into their house?*

There was a small part of her that knew her mind was floating in a haze again, but the fire was so warm and inviting. She was so tired and lost, fog clouded her thoughts, and nothing seemed all that important. Knowing that her thoughts were random and rambling didn't seem to help her focus. She finally managed a small mental happy dance because at least she hadn't melted in a puddle while looking at Mr. Blue Eyes.

She didn't remember how she'd gotten inside and that was troubling. *What happened to the man with the beautiful eyes?* A small movement to her side drew her attention, and it was then that she noticed she was sitting next to him. The very gorgeous, very tall man who had approached her outside was sitting so close if she took a deep breath, they'd be touching. Trying to bring her thoughts back into some semblance of reason, she remembered him talking to her and how everything had seemed to fade into the background, but after that, she didn't remember anything but fog.

Cursing herself for not eating, she struggled to form coherent thoughts. Her counselors had warned that her new habit of forgetting to eat was one of the post-traumatic stress disorder symptoms she needed to focus on dealing with first, but it was a problem she was still struggling to conquer.

Sighing to herself, Bree resolved she was just going to have to surrender and start setting her phone alarm, so she would remember to eat. She slowly began to focus and saw there were actually two gorgeous men staring at her.

Oh, pickle fudge, where did he come from? Oh, hell, maybe these are Catherine's sons? Dandy impression you are making, Sabrina... oh double hell, Bree! I am Bree now! Oh God, I really am hungry.

Looking up at the two men who were watching her so intently, she sighed and wondered how she could have messed this day up any more. Finally realizing both men were watching her as if she was an escaped mental patient, she straightened and found her voice.

"I'm sorry, I guess I should have stopped for a break on the way here. But I'm really not used to mountain driving, and well, to be honest, I was afraid if I stopped, I might not be brave enough to start again." Taking a big breath, she realized she had dropped her gaze to her hands which lay so tightly clasped in her lap, they were beginning to turn white.

Bree's attention was drawn immediately to the tall man who stood in front of her when he asked, "When is the last time you ate anything, sweetheart? You look like you are about to drop. And judging by the fit of your clothes, I'm going to guess you forget to eat fairly often." She couldn't help the small sound of surprise that escaped her lips. Looking up at him, she was surprised to see him smiling.

"How'd I do?"

"Umm... well, pretty good, actually. Oh, nuts, that was really two questions wasn't it? Well, I ate, hmmm, let me think..." She didn't even get to finish when the man standing up pulled a phone from his pocket and spoke sweetly to someone named Selita about a food tray. Promising to send someone to pick it up, he made another quick call, then slipped the phone back into his pocket and returned his attention to her. Watching him warily, she decided action would surely be better than just sitting there like a slug, so she started to stand.

Mr. Blue Eyes settled his hand on her shoulder to keep her from standing up. He was probably worried they'd just have to scoop her up off the floor because it wouldn't have taken a Mensa candidate to see she was running on fumes.

"Why don't you just stay sitting while we all introduce ourselves. I'm Jamie Creed and the fellow standing so tall in front of you, that he's forcing you to strain your neck to see him, is Ethan Jantz."

Ethan must have taken Jamie's hint because he sat on the coffee table in front of them. Then Mr. Blue Eyes, er, Jamie slowly trailed his hand from her shoulder all the way to her hand in what could only be called a sensuous caress that made her shiver with desire.

"Now it's your turn. What's your name, sweetness?"

"Bree. Bree Hart. Mrs. Catherine Lamont sent me." She knew both men were watching her and she still couldn't stop her eyes from automatically moving to her lap again. She stared at her hands, amazed to see Jamie had taken them in his. Carefully unfolding her clenched fingers, he threaded his stronger ones through hers, warming her cold digits. Taking a deep breath, she continued.

"Do you know Mrs. Lamont? She said she would let

her sons know I was on my way. Although to be honest she may not have thought I'd drive in this weather." She shook head and cursed her own foolishness before she quietly added, "It was really dumb I know, but pushing through fear is the only way I've ever been able to conquer it."

ETHAN WAS SURE he would have missed the last of her words if he hadn't been looking right at her, and judging by the look on Creed's face, he was thinking the same thing. The honesty and courage of her statement nearly flattened him. *What on earth could such a beautiful woman have experienced that she'd learned that lesson? Who does she belong to, and why the hell wasn't he taking better care of her?*

Chapter 4

JAMIE HAD GIVEN the tap signal to his earbud when they had first walked through the door, so he knew their conversation was being monitored, and whoever Jantz had left watching the feeds would already be calling the mansion to speak with Alex and Zach Lamont. All they could do was wait until one or both of their bosses showed up. Hopefully, they could get some food in her before the two Doms hit the door.

Even though Alex Lamont had mellowed a lot since he and his brother, Zach married Katarina and become the parents of triplets, Jamie knew the man would still appear damned intimidating to the timid woman sitting next to him. She was obviously trying to keep still enough not to draw any attention despite the fact she was practically vibrating with anxiety. It was almost as if she was trying to make herself invisible.

Adding his observation to the fact she mentioned Denver and Catherine Lamont, Jamie was seeing red flags. Everyone at ShadowDance knew the Lamont matriarch was dedicated to the women's shelters and crisis intervention centers she and her husband had started after their housekeeper Selita entered their lives.

From what Jamie had heard, Daniel and Catherine Lamont had stumbled upon Selita one evening after she'd been badly beaten and left for dead. They'd been leaving a downtown movie theatre and had barely heard her quiet sobs as they'd crossed a dark and filthy alley. The charitable couple had seen to her medical care and helped her free herself from an abusive marriage.

Alex had told them Selita had been sold into marriage as a payment for her safe passage to the United States when she'd been little more than a young girl. Selita had become the nanny and housekeeper for the Lamont family when all three Lamont children were still very young. And to insinuate she was anything but a full-fledged member of the family was to invite all hell to rain down on you. The little ball of fire, known affectionately as the Honduran Tornado, adopted each and every person who joined the team, mothering them just as she did Alex, Zach, and their younger sister, Jenna.

Knowing Selita's story and having seen instances of domestic violence unfold all around him while growing up, Jamie quickly recognized some of those same signs in Bree. He gave an internal head shake and wondered why so many men thought it was their right to harm the women in their lives. He'd always seen women as a blessing, a precious gift to be treasured and kept safe, and anything less was unacceptable.

There was a knock at the door, and Jamie watched as Ethan moved quickly to take the tray from one of the security detail working in and around The Club. When he set it on the table in front of Bree, her eyes widened in surprise. She looked from Jantz to him, then back at the tray.

"How did you get food here so quickly? I mean, thank you, but you really didn't have to do that. I was just planning to speak to Mrs. Lamont's sons, then drive back to town and get something to eat once I'd settled in a motel."

He and Jantz exchanged smiles because they knew Catherine Lamont would not have told her there was a motel in the tiny town of Climax, Colorado because there never had been. They both knew if Catherine had sent her to ShadowDance, there was at least one damned good reason and likely several. Catherine Lamont had a Mensa-worthy IQ and the drive of a dozen steam engines and was adored by everyone who knew her.

Jamie leaned forward to uncover the tray's contents. "Well, since it's here, why don't you help yourself? I know I'll feel better knowing we've taken care of you, and I'm sure Ethan will agree." He didn't miss her quick intake of breath when he'd mentioned taking care of her, and the sweet flush of pink that washed over her cheeks made her even more beautiful.

Watching as she slowly picked up one of the small sandwiches and took a bite, then closed her eyes and groaned in appreciation was a special kind of torture. His mind immediately pictured her with her eyes closed in pleasure, her head thrown back, making that same sound of appreciation while riding his cock. At this rate, he was going to have to excuse himself from the room in order to adjust the raging hard-on that seemed determined to burst through the zipper on his fatigues.

He and Ethan both watched quietly as she ate the better part of the meal Selita had prepared for her before she finally leaned back, looking for all intents and purposes like a well-satisfied cat, ready for a nice nap. Jamie smiled to himself, thinking the bosses were likely watching the feeds and were simply waiting for her to get fully settled before making themselves known. Both Alex and Zach were skilled interrogators thanks to years of Special Forces training, but everyone knew it was teammate, Mitch Grayson who usually got the most valuable information.

Grayson was a strong empath, and his ability to pick up the thoughts and emotions of those around him was more often than not unnervingly accurate. Right on cue, Jamie's earbud crackled to life, and he heard Grayson's laughing voice.

"Aww, that's so sweet. Thinking about me, Creed?" When Jamie merely glared in the direction of one of the room's several security cameras, Mitch continued, "She's hiding something, big Bro, and just FYI the name Bree Hart is so clean it squeaks and shines."

Ethan knew immediately his friend was saying it was a created identity. No one's real identity was that "scrubbed," so either she worked for one of the government's alphabet agencies or she was in some sort of witness protection program, and from what he'd observed, his money was on the latter. He leaned forward and moved the tray back enough, so Jantz could sit in front of her again. Just as Ethan sat down, the door opened, and Alex and Zach Lamont strode into the room.

BREE WAS GETTING so sleepy she could barely keep her eyes open. She couldn't believe how much she'd eaten, but it had all tasted so wonderful, and she'd been so terribly hungry, she'd essentially attacked the meal like a starved animal. She felt herself begin to slide into the dark pools of her memories, remembering the unending hunger of her captivity. At first, she'd been too repulsed by what they'd brought her to eat, then later she'd been too terrified to eat it for fear it was laced with drugs or worse.

Finally, deciding that being embarrassed by her fatigue just wasn't worth the effort, she settled her back against the soft leather of the sofa and let the warmth of the fire wash over her. She was just about to slide off into blissful sleep when she heard the door open. When she finally managed to open her eyes, she was stunned by the men entering the room.

Bree remembered Catherine mentioning her sons were twins, but her friend hadn't mentioned how handsome they were or that they were virtual mirror images of one another. There was no doubt these were the Lamont brothers, no indeed. After meeting Catherine's husband, Daniel, Bree would have recognized his sons anywhere. *Holy crap! How does anyone tell them apart?*

The medical professional in her immediately began cataloging details, hoping to figure out a way to tell Alex and Zach Lamont apart. She wondered if their mother's description of their personalities would help her ask them for their help. Just thinking about the real reason, she was here sent shivers through her entire body. Was she brave enough to face her own desires? Taking a deep breath and straightening her spine, she decided it was finally time to find out.

Chapter 5

ALEX LAMONT HAD just finished speaking with his mother when he'd gotten the call they had a visitor. He and his brother had watched her on the security feeds for several minutes longer than they'd needed because it had been very interesting to watch the byplay between Creed and Jantz. He and Zach had discussed their friends recently and wondered how long it would be before they met their own woman, and from all appearances, that moment had finally arrived.

Stepping forward, he held out his hand and introduced himself. "Hello, Ms. Hart, I'm Alex Lamont. And that fellow standing over there is my much less attractive brother, Zach." He smiled when his comment seemed to put her more at ease, which had been exactly what he'd hoped it would do.

When they had first entered the room, she had jumped to her feet, and Alex had wondered for just an instant if she was planning to flee but had quickly decided it was likely a simple point of etiquette for her. That action alone told him she was either raised in a very strict military or religious home, or perhaps, she'd spent a lot of time in European boarding schools. His mother hadn't given them all the details of her background, choosing instead to focus on what she viewed as the young woman's "current needs."

Zach stepped forward and nodded his head toward her and smiled. Alex was relieved to note she seemed to relax even further at his brother's acknowledgment. Everyone knew Zach was the easier of the two of them to approach, so Alex usually greeted people first. They had discovered it kept guests and business associates and particularly women from thinking they could deal exclusively with Zach. Alex watched her closely as Zach spoke.

"Hi, I'm Zach, it's nice to meet you. Mom was just telling us to expect you. We're glad you made it safely." Glancing at the empty tray, he added, "And that these two yahoos saw fit to be hospitable and feed you. I'm guessing it was a grueling drive, particularly for someone not accustomed to mountain roads."

Alex saw her eyes flash and knew she must have been terrified by the drive. The roads leading into Climax were filled with switchbacks and steep grades that would be hazardous to navigate in the type of storm that had gone through earlier that day.

Alex moved back and positioned himself, so he was leaning against the mantle of the fireplace. Jantz had stepped to Bree's side. When he looked up at Alex, he had shaken his head and rolled his eyes. Alex knew it was his friend's way of letting him know every team member in the room and watching knew his pose was "deceptively casual" even though it was a well-practiced position. Knowing his brother as well as he knew himself, Alex was sure Zach was quickly reading the body language of every person in the room.

Zach smiled when he motioned for Bree to return to her seat and Creed quickly sat down so close, their thighs were touching. Alex stayed back and just watched as Zach pulled one of the straight-backed chairs over closer before sitting down, so he would be on the woman's level, then leaned forward, ensuring their conversation appeared as intimate as possible. Alex had to give his brother credit, his skills at putting people at ease far surpassed his own, so he just stood back and listened as Zach spoke in soothing tones to their guest.

"Ms. Hart, our mom told us briefly why she sent you here. Are you comfortable having this conversation with everyone in the room? If you prefer, my brother and I can arrange to speak with you privately."

Alex suppressed a smile. No doubt, they'd have to answer all of Creed and Jantz's questions later, but right now, both he and his brother were both more concerned with her comfort level than the two men watching over her like hawks.

Bree took a deep, steadying breath, and Alex knew she was trying to figure out who she felt the most comfortable with. He was impressed when she quickly seemed to refocus before answering.

"First of all, please call me Bree. Ms. Hart sounds so terribly formal, and after all, I've heard about all of you, well, I guess I kind of feel like I know you already." She stared at her hands for long seconds before she continued, "I don't really know how to answer that question because I don't know exactly what your mom told you, but I'm assuming she was pretty clear since you asked me... oh dear, I'm making a mess of this." Glancing up at Zach, she seemed to relax at his expression.

Alex spoke to her in quiet, measured tones. "Bree, we are accustomed to frank discussions and a wide variety of topics." When she gave him a puzzled look, he smiled and finished, "What I'm trying to say is I'm absolutely positive there is nothing you can say to shock any of the people in this room. The question my brother is dancing around is will you be comfortable having this discussion in the presence of men I am sure you must be aware are attracted to you?"

BREE KNEW SHE had better just suck it up if she was serious about learning more about the BDSM lifestyle and exploring what it might hold for her. The only way she was going to have any chance of success was to be willing to do things that were outside of her comfort zone. She wanted to shake her head at her own naivety. *Geez, "comfort zone" implies you have a fudging clue which you don't. Holy hell, look what a mess you've landed yourself in this time.* Finally, taking a deep breath and then looking at Alex and Zach, she looked directly at Zach.

"Do you think it would be okay if they stayed?" Zach's warm smile told her what she needed to know, but it was his kind words that warmed her heart.

"Sweetness, you can be completely open with any of us. We'll answer your questions as best we can. But in truth, I have a feeling you'd be more at ease talking to them without either my brother or me in the room. If I told you that both Alex and I have full confidence not only in both of these men's ability to guide you but also in their willingness, perhaps even their eagerness to do so, would that help?"

Bree couldn't help the small chuckle that erupted from her and shook her head, wondering again how on earth she managed to get herself in such situations.

"Yes, I believe that would help. Both you and your brother are married to the same woman, isn't that right?" When Zach and Alex both nodded she continued. "And you have small children, correct?" Again, at their nods, she said, "To be honest, I don't know your wife, and I'm not that comfortable asking these questions of married men." She turned to the man sitting next to her. "Are you or your friend Ethan married?"

She saw Jamie Creed try to suppress his smile and assumed it was because he was quickly figuring out why she'd come to The ShadowDance Club. When he finally answered, she felt drawn in by his voice alone.

"No, Bree, we are both single. We are also both Doms, in case that is your next question." He smiled when he saw her eyes widen. She knew her breathing hitched and the small gasp she had tried to rein in had escaped despite her best efforts.

STANDING TO THE side, Ethan was watching every nuance of her behavior, gestures, and voice. One of the most significant skills for a sniper was learning to read body language because missing even the smallest "tell" could mean the difference in saving, not only your own life but also the lives of your spotter and teammates as well. He watched as Zach leaned forward and grasped her hands in his.

"Bree, even though we are married and have been blessed with the cutest kids on the planet, doesn't mean we don't look out for the members of our club. Making sure the ShadowDance Club is a safe place for each of our members, particularly the submissives, to explore and enjoy their sexuality is always our priority. We will be happy to help in whatever way you are most comfortable."

Ethan watched as Alex stepped forward, and when Bree turned her attention to him he saw her initial hesitation. He also knew the instant she'd realized even though his demeanor seemed to have a harder edge, his eyes shone with concern. Alex squatted down to speak to the beauty sitting in front of him.

"Bree, our mother knew we would make sure you had the opportunity to have your questions answered in a safe environment. She charged us with making certain you were in good hands, and I can assure you, we've known both Jamie and Ethan for a long time and would trust them with our lives."

He and Ethan both laughed, and he saw Alex's smile before he shook his head and added.

"They are laughing because we *have* trusted them with our lives on several occasions as we were all on the same Special Forces team. So perhaps, it would be more meaningful if I told you I would trust them with the lives of our beloved Katarina and our children."

Seeing how his eyes softened at the mention of his wife and children was heartwarming, and Ethan was sure that hadn't been lost on Bree when he noticed she'd relaxed even more. Zach stood and smiled down at her before turning his attention to him and Jamie.

"We'll be expecting you all for dinner tonight. Explain to Bree, clearly, what she might expect and make sure she is dressed appropriately. Begin as you intend to go, gentlemen." At their nods, he added, "Also, we'll be moving her things into Jenna's old suite, so please explain the security system to her. We'll also arrange for her car to be secured in the garage."

Alex watched the realization they were planning on her staying in their home rather than in a motel move over her expression.

"Wait. I can't impose on your wife and family. She'll think horribly of me if you put her in that position. You can't expect her to fix extra for dinner this late in the day? I'll just drive back into that small town down the mountain and find a nice bed & breakfast or motel room."

He didn't even try to hide his smile when she started frantically looking from Alex to Zach, then to both Jamie and himself as if she was expecting one of them to back her up. Since they were all grinning at her, Ethan was fairly certain she'd figured out they were all a lost cause.

While Alex had seemed relaxed and approachable a few minutes ago, his response to Bree's answer had reminded him of velvet-covered steel. This was the Alex Lamont Jamie was accustomed to seeing and hearing. His voice was pitched low and seemed almost frighteningly calm.

"I'll tell you what, come have dinner with us. Meet everyone, then if you still feel like you'll be imposing, we'll see what we can do about finding you other accommodations. How's that sound?"

Ethan didn't doubt, despite the fact she had just met the man, Bree would know Alex's question wasn't really a question at all.

"Well, I have to say, it's easy to see your mother's steel will in you," she chuckled. "Once she decided I should visit ShadowDance, she refused to take no for an answer. There was no backing out. That woman is a force of nature, I tell you."

Ethan watched as she obviously tried to calculate her

odds of winning this argument and was immensely pleased when her posture showed her acquiescence.

"I'd love to join your family for dinner if you're sure adding another person won't be an inconvenience. And I'd be happy to help your wife with the preparations. Would that help?"

Alex and Zach shared a look, then both laughed out loud before Alex answered, "No, sweetness, I'm afraid our wife and sister are not allowed to cook. As a matter of fact, I believe Trace and Tori Bartell will be here this evening also, and I can assure you Tori is not allowed to even go *in a* kitchen. Be sure to ask her about her neighborhood fire department in Houston inviting her to eat dinner with them each evening, so they could skip their nightly runs to her apartment."

All the men in the room laughed, and Ethan wanted to tell Bree she was seeing a bit of Alex Lamont most people never got to see—hell, even his friends didn't see *this* Alex very often.

Alex was usually described as "harsh," and his reputation as a hard-assed former Special Forces soldier with a cutting-edge business sense and a take-no-prisoners attitude was well earned. While Zach was usually described as the more affable one, those who knew the brothers well would tell you, he was every bit as dominating as his twin.

FIGURING HE HAD let the bosses handle things long enough, he decided it was time to move this little "meet and greet party" along. Truth be told Jamie could hardly wait to get Bree alone and start finding out, in excruciating detail, exactly what she was interested in learning. He found himself absolutely mesmerized by her.

There was something about her that called to him. It was as if his soul recognized her, but he was sure he wasn't going to be able to figure it out until some of his blood managed to make its way back to his brain. Judging from the raging hard-on he'd had since first laying eyes on Bree, that wasn't going to be happening anytime soon. Hell, it was a fucking miracle he was still conscious with so much blood pooled below his waist.

Standing, he held his hand out for her and was pleased when she placed her fingers in his. "Bree, why don't you let Ethan and I show you around a bit? We'll let the bosses get back to their family, and they'll let Kat know you'll be joining us for dinner." He raised a hand, halting her when she started to ask a question. "I promise you, there is no reason for you to help Selita, but we'll stop by the kitchen, so you can hear that from her yourself." Enclosing her tiny hand in his much larger one, he nodded to Ethan, and they set out down the hall.

"Can you tell me, please, who is Selita?" Bree's question sounded so "proper," Jamie almost laughed. He watched as she looked around, taking in the sudden shift in the décor. He knew she would have noticed the hall she was being led down was reminiscent of a Middle Ages castle, and even though it was beautiful, it was also quite intimidating for newcomers.

This time it was Ethan who answered. "Selita is affectionately known as the Honduran Tornado, but is, in fact, the Lamont family's longtime housekeeper and cook extraordinaire. She adopts everyone who enters her realm, and just so you know, the reason we were all grinning like fools about your concern over adding another person to a meal is dinner here is an event each night. It is not uncommon for there to be thirty people at the table, and I assure you, Selita is thrilled with every person she gets to feed."

Jamie watched as Bree's expression opened, and the worry lines at the corners of her eyes faded. She obviously hadn't missed his and Ethan's silent communication and he didn't want her second-guessing her decision to allow them to become her escorts, so he quickly opened the door in front of them. He knew the surprise that awaited her on the other side would be a full-meal-deal distraction.

He and Jantz watched her reaction as they stepped from the building. She stopped dead in her tracks and turned in a slow circle, trying to take in the beautiful garden area they'd entered. He heard her softly whisper that she felt like Dorothy in *The Wizard of Oz* waking up from the bleak black and white of Kansas to find herself in the colorful splendor of Oz. He was sure she hadn't even realized she had spoken her thoughts aloud.

Chapter 6

"OH MY GOD in heaven, this has to be one of the most beautiful places I've ever seen." Bree knew she was standing there gaping as she tried to take it all in. She was trying to imprint everything to her memory. It was a habit she'd learned during her brief childhood visits to the many beautiful locations her family had visited over the years. Since her parents were often assigned to worst hellholes on the planet, she'd learned early on to take in every detail and nuance when they visited a beautiful location, so she could *escape* there in her mind later.

Bree's attention was focused on the trees and landscaping in general, but she didn't miss all the security monitoring equipment that was, oddly enough, right out in plain view. *I wonder why that equipment is so clearly visible? That seems out of sync with everything else I see. Apparently, the security staff wants The Club's members to know they are protected. I'm not sure why that surprises me, but it does. Hmm. I hear water running, maybe a waterfall? Oh, that's going to be my favorite part, I already know it. Catherine was right, this place is magical. I hope she's right about the rest as well, I've been lost too long.*

CREED AND JANTZ had stepped to the side as soon as they had realized their beautiful charge was drifting in thought and blissfully unaware she was speaking out loud. Jamie knew it was their endless Special Forces and black ops training kicking in as they faded seamlessly into the background to watch and listen. The rules about learning everything possible about a target made acquisition easier, and those constructs were as easily applied to a target you were taking out as to one you planned to keep.

Their teammates had often commented on the fact their tandem movements seemed almost orchestrated, but in truth, they had worked together so often, they fell into pattern easily. Using hand signals to communicate, they had agreed she was processing aloud and had become so focused on her own thoughts, she had forgotten they were even near.

Watching and listening to Bree's observations and ramblings was interesting but raised more questions than they answered. Jamie agreed with her in that the gardens behind The ShadowDance Club were spectacular. The entire area was bordered by The ShadowDance Club, the mansion where the Lamont family lived, and the new addition Colt and Jenna Matthews had recently built. The surrounding forest backed the horseshoe-shaped structure. The entire garden area was a scenic wonder.

When Colt, a former team leader, married Alex and Zach Lamont's younger sister, the addition to the mansion had provided the final line of weather protection, and the gardens had flourished as a result. Heated by natural thermal springs, the temperatures were tolerable during all but the most extreme winter conditions.

The waterfall was indeed something to behold, and Jamie could hardly wait to show it to her. It had been crafted of native stone, but the lighting was its most spectacular feature. Both the lights and the water jets could be synched to music, making it a favorite "Girls' Night In" location. Those parties always resulted in naked women dancing in the water to Kat's favorite country tunes, and the bosses inevitably confiscated all the security discs, much to the frustration of their security team.

Bree finally seemed to realize they were standing back, waiting for her to finish her observations, and Jamie saw her blush when she realized she'd been speaking aloud. Looking between them, she finally spoke, her words soft and stilted.

"Oh my, I'm so sorry. I was just overcome by the beauty the Lamonts have created here. Which one of them is the landscaper? Or did they have someone do it professionally?"

Ethan stepped forward and answered. "It was a family effort and has been completed in stages and improved upon several times. The most recent changes were made for both Alex and Zach's wedding to Katarina and enhanced again for their younger sister Jenna's wedding to Colt Matthews. The new addition you see across the way is where Colt and Jenna live. You'll meet them tonight at dinner. Colt is the Chief of Security for The ShadowDance Club and all the land surrounding it that is owned by the Lamont family."

"Oh goodness, it's wonderful the siblings all live so close. I know Catherine mentioned her daughter had recently gotten married and lived near her brothers, but I didn't realize it was quite this close." Her voice dropped to a near whisper and Jamie wasn't sure her words had been spoken to them or to herself when she added, "It must be so wonderful to have siblings you love and respect. I can't even say how often I wished for someone to share my life with." The lonely expression that moved over her face almost had Jamie stepping forward to wrap her in his warm embrace.

Deciding it was time to break her melancholy, Jamie stepped forward and secured her small hand in the bend of his elbow and began moving toward the deck along the back of the mansion.

"Come on, beautiful, let us introduce you to Selita, and you can see for yourself that you won't be intruding." Jamie knew Ethan was close behind Bree. Since they had worked and played together for so long, they could easily anticipate the other's actions to within a fraction of a second. Leading Bree through the door of the breakfast nook and into the kitchen, he smiled as he heard Selita chattering away to both Alex and Zach in Spanish.

Neither he nor Ethan had to wonder for long if Bree was bilingual when she giggled as Selita threatened to paddle the men's backsides if they didn't get out of her kitchen. Bree leaned over closer to Jamie's ear.

"I think seeing that tiny woman paddle men who are twice her size might be worth the price of admission," she whispered. "Can we watch?" As if realizing the familiarity with which she'd spoken to him, she seemed to tense before dropping her gaze to the floor. "Oh God, I can't believe I said that. It was inappropriate, and I'm really sorry. But she is so funny. And what did she mean when she called them big galoshes?"

Both he and Ethan laughed out loud at her question. Then quickly explained when they noted her face flush in embarrassment. Jamie watched as Ethan spoke close to her ear.

"No, Love, we weren't laughing at you but at the situation. And frankly, it was refreshing to see it through your eyes. I daresay, we must be getting desensitized to the humor of it, and that's a pity."

Ethan turned Bree to face him, placing his hands on either side of her face and moving his thumbs over her high cheekbones in soft, stroking caresses. Jamie was always amazed when Ethan's Dom persona surfaced for the first time with a woman. Their reactions were varied but always intense. He was pleased to see Bree was no exception. Standing to the side, Jamie watched as her pupils dilated, and her breathing hitched. *Oh yeah, you felt that shift in our interaction clear to your soul didn't you, Chère?*

Knowing Ethan was beginning with her, Jamie stepped up behind her, pressing himself flush against her soft curves, and placed his hands on her waist. Ethan explained Selita's habit of butchering American slang and expressions, and Jamie felt her relax beneath his touch when she realized her question was perfectly reasonable, and no one would be surprised or offended by it. Together, the three of them reasoned Selita had likely meant to call the men "big galoots," and they had enjoyed a shared laugh before turning back to the chaos the Lamonts were causing in the kitchen.

Chapter 7

ETHAN KNEW BOTH Alex and Zach had seen them enter the house, so he was fairly certain their antics were for Bree's benefit. He appreciated their efforts to put her at ease. As they stepped into the kitchen, Selita looked up and smiled sweetly.

"Oh, Ethan, Jamie, you bring a beautiful woman to meet your sugar-goat mama?" Wiping her hands on her apron, she stepped forward and held out her hand to Bree. "I am so glad to meet you, are you going to make these two straight?"

Alex started coughing and Zach laughed out loud at Selita's words. Ethan glared at them both before turning to Selita.

"Mama Selita, I believe the phrase you are looking for is 'straighten them out.' The way you said it implies you think Creed and I are gay."

Selita looked at Ethan with wide eyes and then laughed. "Dios. I know you are not liking to do that funny stuff with men. No, that was not my meaning at all." She turned back to Bree and smiled. "I am so happy you are here. Mrs. Catherine called and said she was sending a beautiful woman and here you are. Miss Jenna's suite is all ready for you, and if you are needing anything you just tell me. No telling what these men would be getting for you if you asked them. Sometimes, they not using their pumpkins, you know what I mean?"

Ethan heard the other three men trying to suppress their laughter as he smiled down at Selita, vowing to be sure she received some sort of special gift for making Bree feel so welcome.

"Thank you, Selita, you are a wonderful hostess, and I'm sure Bree appreciates all you have done."

Bree had been standing in front of Selita with a wide-eyed look of puzzlement that made her look adorable. Ethan moved his hand to her back, and that small contact seemed to bring her back to the moment.

"Oh, I do... very much... I mean... I appreciate everything you have done. Is there anything I can do to help you get ready for dinner? I feel just awful about barging in and eating you out of house and home right off the bat. The sandwich tray you sent earlier was wonderful. Now, you point out how I can help, and I'll do whatever you need."

Selita smiled at Bree but then looked at Ethan and Jamie. "You need to be keeping this one, she is a... oh ¡*maldita sea*! What is the word for the box of gold?"

Alex stepped forward and answered, his love and respect for the tiny woman plain to see in his eyes. "Selita, I believe you are saying that Bree is a treasure, and we all agree with you. Remember, we all speak Spanish, so trying to slip that 'damn' in unnoticed won't work. Now, if you don't have anything for her to help with, I'm sure she'd like to have a chance to freshen up before dinner. Jamie and Ethan will show her to her suite. My brother and I have already taken her things up for her. Now, we need to get back up and help Katarina get the children settled, so she has time to rest a bit before dinner."

Ethan was pleased when Selita stepped forward and

hugged Bree tightly. When the little dynamo released the sweet woman, he was already starting to think of as theirs, he heard her murmur something in Spanish before telling them if Bree wanted to help, she could come downstairs a few minutes before seven and help carry food to the table.

After Selita had returned to the kitchen, Ethan and Jamie each took one of Bree's hands and made their way up the wide staircase pointing out various features of the Lamonts' home along the way. Ethan knew Jamie was watching each and every reaction, facial expression, and subtlety of Bree's behavior.

Even though they were both Doms, their approaches and styles were vastly different. They had always figured that was why they worked so well together. Both of them assumed their complementary styles would be a major plus for the woman they shared their life with. The tingling sensation that raced up his arm each time he touched Bree told Ethan, after years of searching the globe for her, their woman had been all but hand-delivered by Catherine Lamont.

Leading her through the door and into the suite, Ethan turned to watch her reaction when she heard Jamie lock the door behind them. He watched as her breathing became shallow, and her hands started to shake. Apprehension was good but real fear was not. Looking over at Creed, he gave his friend a quick nod. Jamie Creed's easygoing Cajun charm would work to their advantage, and Ethan knew it was time for a bit of tag-team play.

JAMIE STEPPED UP so close to Bree, he knew she would be

able to feel the heat radiating from his body and considering his state of arousal, it might well scorch her. He turned her so that she was facing him and when he ran his fingertips up her arm, he felt her shiver.

"*Ma jolie*, are you cold?"

"No. I'm just, well, I know Mrs. Lamont said I would be safe here and well, I'm trying to not fall back into old habits and fears... but..." Jamie took the last small step and pulled her easily into his chest and wrapped his arms around her and just held her. When he felt her tears dampen his shirt, he nearly lost the last bit of his control. He was shocked by his overwhelming urge to care for the woman clinging to him as if he was her lifeline. When she finally pulled herself back and looked up into his face, the vulnerability in her eyes brought every protective instinct he had bubbling right to the surface.

BREE WAS SHOCKED. *French. He spoke French to me... just like...* She immediately flashed back to the scene she had relived a thousand times. She'd awakened to the feeling of being carried, wrapped in the warm embrace of a man she didn't recognize, but she'd instinctively known his strength was gentle. And while the strength she felt wrapped around her now didn't seem threatening, the soldier who had rescued her had radiated a fierce rage. She had known he wasn't angry at her, but rather his anger was *for* her.

As he was running away from the small camp where she'd been held, he must have sensed she had awakened because he'd reassured her she was safe... and he'd called her *Chère*. She had recognized it as the French endearment spoken between lovers. On some deep level of consciousness, she had wondered why an American soldier wouldn't just say "sweetheart." Later, she'd later learned it was a word often used in the Cajun South.

She had thought of him often, wishing she'd had the strength to say thank you. By the time she had recovered enough to consider trying to contact him, her entire world had fallen apart. When she had discovered everything she had always believed about her life and her family was built on lies, she'd begun wondering if she'd stepped through Alice's looking glass. While people looked the same from one angle, everything had shifted, and it all appeared entirely new.

Sabrina Gillette had ceased to exist, and Bree Hart had been born. The damage her captors had done while beating her for information about her parents' involvement in international espionage had required extensive restorative plastic surgery, and there were still times she looked in the mirror barely recognizing the woman staring back at her. She had been fortunate most of the work had been done by lasers which had shortened her recovery time considerably and left very little evidence she'd been injured.

She'd been completely devastated when she'd been forced to give up the life she'd had before her kidnapping and refused to even speak with her parents again. Despite their repeated attempts to contact her, even recently, she had steadfastly refused any contact. They had cost her everything, and she wasn't ready to forgive them for all the years of lies and all she'd lost.

Bree finally realized the man holding her had asked her a question and his voice had drawn her back to the present. "I'm sorry, what did you ask?" She knew she had likely looked totally disconnected for a bit—others had described to her how she would stare off into space for several minutes, lost in the flashbacks and memories.

The few people she had spent time with frequently commented it seemed to take her several long minutes to fight her way back to the surface of her own consciousness. But this time, she felt like she'd been pulled over the edge by this man... there was something so hauntingly familiar about his countenance, his voice, his soul... it all seemed to call to her, and she fought to figure out why.

Seeing the concern reflected in his blue eyes brought her fully back to the moment. Bree realized Jamie had stepped back, so he could frame her face with his large hands. Using the calloused pads of his thumbs, he wiped away her tears. The reassuring press of his fingers against her scalp where his fingers were threaded through her hair grounded her with their soothing pressure. The peace she felt at his touch reminded her again of her Cajun angel.

"Baby, I don't know where you went, but I have to tell you, I'd rather you didn't venture there again. The sadness and fear I saw in your face are going to haunt me until we can replace that memory with something more pleasant. You reminded me of someone else for a moment, someone I helped a year ago." Jamie cleared his throat.

I'm not going fall into that memory. It's time to lighten the mood.

Chapter 8

JAMIE SMILED DOWN at her, his words a gentle challenge. "Now that you're back, I want you to tell us why Catherine Lamont sent you to ShadowDance." He saw her eyes flash with arousal and curiosity just an instant before her face flushed a deep crimson. "Ah, now there's a beautiful sight, don't you agree, Master Ethan?" He saw her sharp intake of breath more than heard it when she'd registered his words. "So, Bree, you understand why Master Ethan and I are referred to in that way, don't you?" He'd seen the recognition in her eyes just before she'd dropped her gaze to the floor.

Oh yes, ma Chère, you are definitely a submissive.

"Yes. Well, I do understand some, I mean, well, I've read some things. Oh blast, I'm messing this up royally, aren't I?" The more she had spoken, the softer her words had gotten and while neither he nor Ethan wanted her to shout her answers, they needed to be able to hear her.

Jamie made sure his words were a quiet, but steely command. "Bree, look at me." When she finally raised her eyes to his he continued, "I want you to remember, this is just a preliminary discussion, alright? Ethan and I need to understand what you are interested in exploring. I'm assuming that's why Catherine sent you here, is that correct?" When she nodded her head, he smiled. "Ordinarily, we won't allow you to simply nod or shake your head in answer to our questions, for several reasons. The most important of those is that we'll need to be sure you fully understand the question or command, and we'll also want to make sure we've gotten your answer right."

While he'd been speaking to her, he'd been slowly leading her to the small sofa positioned in front of one of the floor-to-ceiling windows with a panoramic view of the gardens. He knew Ethan was standing nearby, but his friend had sensed Bree's insecurity and backed off. Jamie had always had better luck drawing out a newbie sub or helping an insecure one feel more comfortable when she didn't have enough confidence or experience to deal with the Ethan's more alpha style of dominance.

Ethan and Jamie had always felt they would be able to bring a great balance to a relationship if they shared a woman. During their long hours of "hurry up and wait" which was the hallmark of so many of their missions, they'd had hundreds of hours to discuss exactly how they envisioned the logistics of a polyamorous relationship working. Their friends had teased them about planning out everything to the ninth degree, reminding them they were forgetting one key element—the woman.

Jamie sat and pulled a surprised Bree down onto his lap. He didn't say anything for a few minutes, just sat quietly, looking out the window and rubbing his hand in slow circles over her lower back until he felt her begin to relax.

"That's it, sweetness, settle a bit, then we'll talk some more." He wanted her to understand they weren't going to pressure her for any information or for sex. It was obvious she was nervous and building a solid foundation of trust was critical.

He hadn't forgotten the comment she'd made to Alex and Zach about their mother telling her she would be "safe" at ShadowDance, and he knew Catherine Lamont well enough to know that she didn't make random comments nor did she do anything without a reason. If she'd sent Bree to them, then they'd damned well keep her safe.

SITTING ON JAMIE Creed's lap was unnerving at first, but Bree eventually began to relax when he didn't pressure her to answer any questions. After one particularly grueling flashback, Bree had confided in Catherine that she had just begun learning about Dominant/submissive relationships when she'd been kidnapped, and she hadn't found the courage to begin exploring again. When Catherine heard about everything she had endured, she had held her, and they'd cried together. Bree had entrusted her with details she hadn't even shared with her counselors. In other words, Bree had quite literally entrusted Catherine Lamont with her life.

She'd watched the woman whose generosity provided shelter and programs for abused women in Denver as she'd consoled, encouraged, guided, taught, and laughed with victims of all ages. Catherine's unconditional love and support for those in need had been one of the most inspirational things Bree had ever witnessed. So, when Catherine Lamont assured Bree she would be safe at ShadowDance, that her sons and their team of black ops soldiers could keep her safe while she explored all things BDSM, she'd decided to take a chance and put herself in their hands.

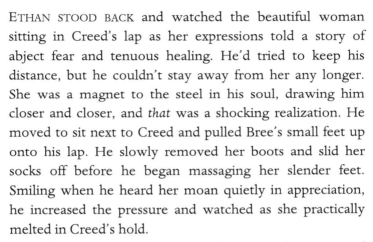

ETHAN STOOD BACK and watched the beautiful woman sitting in Creed's lap as her expressions told a story of abject fear and tenuous healing. He'd tried to keep his distance, but he couldn't stay away from her any longer. She was a magnet to the steel in his soul, drawing him closer and closer, and *that* was a shocking realization. He moved to sit next to Creed and pulled Bree's small feet up onto his lap. He slowly removed her boots and slid her socks off before he began massaging her slender feet. Smiling when he heard her moan quietly in appreciation, he increased the pressure and watched as she practically melted in Creed's hold.

When he started moving his hands slowly up around her ankles and over her calves trying to ease the muscle fatigue, he knew she'd have after driving for so long, he said, "Love, one of the things you need to know about the dinner you are about to attend is the submissives dress according to the rules of The Club." He watched her eyes widen and saw the pulse at the base of her neck quicken. "We won't enforce each and every rule tonight because we don't have time to adequately explain everything or discuss your hard and soft limits. Nor do we know as much about your background as I think we may need to."

Ethan had been watching her very carefully, and even then, he wasn't sure he'd have noticed it if he hadn't been touching her, but it had been there, the reaction he'd known was coming. The barely discernable stiffening of her muscles she'd obviously tried very hard to suppress. In all his years of studying body language, he'd never seen anyone work as hard to camouflage their reactions as this woman. Those self-monitoring skills are learned and practiced by people in their line of work as operators or those in some type of protection program. He'd bet every cent the Lamonts paid him this past year he knew which one of those Bree Hart was.

"Since it is getting close to dinner time, we just have a few questions for you before we let you get ready. First, how many sexual partners have you had?" Ethan knew he needed to get right to the point before she had a chance to build up any of the defenses he sensed she ordinarily employed. When she gasped and tried to pull back, he was glad he had gone straight to the heart of it. "No. Leave your legs right where they are, Love." Tightening his grip on her legs, he kept his words pitched low but made sure the command in his tone was unmistakable.

"Um, well, I... oh my, this is harder to discuss with someone I don't really know than I thought it would be. Mercy, why did I think I could do this? I thought I'd be able to use the anonymity to my advantage, but..."

Both Ethan and Jamie watched as she stared at her hands for several seconds before looking up. Ethan wasn't sure he'd ever seen a sub with as many emotions chasing across her face as the sweet one on Creed's lap. Whoever had taught her to monitor her body language had failed miserably at helping her mask her facial expressions. He watched as she tried to form the words to answer his question, but they just didn't seem to be making their way from intention to action.

Creed looked up at Ethan and smiled, and there wasn't any doubt in Ethan's mind his friend was as captivated by her as he was. Ethan smiled, deciding to make it a bit easier for her.

"Let's try this. Have you ever had sex, Bree?" He wasn't surprised to see her immediately lower her eyes and shake her head back and forth slowly. "Okay. Now, how old are you?"

"I'm twenty-four."

"Okay. Just so you know, Master Creed is twenty-nine, and I am twenty-eight. Now, what is your occupation, Love?" None of her reactions had been a big surprise until now. When her eyes filled with tears and sadness swept over her in visible waves, he was stunned. Of all the questions he'd ever asked a sub, he'd never had one react like this to an inquiry about what they did for a living. He waited, never letting his eyes move from her, and in his peripheral vision, he saw Jamie was studying her as well.

They watched as Bree took a couple of deep, steadying breaths before whispering, "I do not have a career at this time. I recently had to give up something I loved very much, and I haven't found... I haven't decided, well, I just don't know what to do now." When she finally brought her gaze up to theirs, there were tears streaming down her cheeks and the bleakness surrounding her had them both wrapping their arms around her.

"We'll explore that more later, but for now, up you go." Ethan helped her to her feet and turned her to face Creed. "Take your shower and get ready for dinner. We'll lay out your clothes on the bed while you are in the shower."

Jamie stepped forward and cupped her cheek in his hand. "Wear what we lay out for you, nothing more and nothing less. Is that clear? We'll be back in fifteen minutes to get you. Do not leave the suite without us. Now, let's get you into the bathroom and into that shower."

Ethan watched as Jamie gently pressed her lower back,

guiding her to the large en suite bath. Maintaining physical contact whenever possible was critical at this stage, not only for the Dom but for the submissive as well.

It was easy to see Bree's need for physical contact was greater because of her feelings of vulnerability, and they'd make a concentrated effort to make certain she felt their touch as often as possible. Ethan had known Doms who used denial of touch as a way to *manage* their sub's behavior—and the plan always failed miserably. How did anyone who professed to be a sexual Dominant not fully understand touch was a basic human need? Hell, the denial of physical contact could actually lead to death in infants.

"After dinner," Jamie continued in the same matter-of-fact tone of voice, "we'll come back up here and play for a bit. During dinner, you are going to meet a lot of people, but don't worry about keeping everyone straight at this point. What you do need to remember is that we will be touching you during the meal. When we sit down, you'll spread your legs apart and leave them that way, hooking your feet on the outside of the chair legs. If we move your clothing aside, you will leave it the way we've positioned it. Oh, and sweetness, don't expend a lot of energy worrying about what the others will think because I can assure you, every submissive at the table is going to be experiencing the same thing or more." Both Ethan and Jamie chuckled when her panic faded a bit as Jamie directed her to step through the door of the enormous bathroom and shut the door.

"She's ours, you know. There is something about her that calls to me, and I can see you feel the same. Let's go get ready. I haven't looked forward to dinner this much in a very long time."

Ethan couldn't have agreed more.

Chapter 9

BREE WAS BUSY in the kitchen helping Selita. Catherine had been right, the small woman was an absolute hoot to spend time with. Bree hadn't learned to cook in a real kitchen because her family had always lived in relatively primitive conditions. Except for her college years in London, she hadn't even lived in a place with indoor plumbing before moving to Denver. As she looked around the kitchen, she was amazed by the incredible beauty surrounding her. And the gadgets... oh heavens, there were so many fascinating gadgets, she'd nearly been derailed wanting to explore them all. She'd laughed and told Selita she didn't even know what most of those interesting little appliances *did*.

Helping set the table had been an eye-opening experience in itself. *Mercy, do they really feed this many people every night?* When people started congregating in the open dining area, she was introduced to so many people, she feared she'd never learn all their names. Alex and Zach Lamont's wife Katarina had blown into the kitchen just a few minutes after Bree and had immediately made her feel like an old friend rather than a guest. The little whirlwind had insisted Bree call her Kat and had promised to arrange a "Girls' Night In" margarita party in the near future. Kat had barely whispered the words but had still received a scathing look from Alex while Zach stood behind his brother and winked at his wife. Their easy interaction helped Bree feel at home, and she was sure that was their intention.

Alex's easy command of the room was clearly evident when he moved to seat his wife and everyone else immediately took their seats. Bree was carrying the last tray into the dining area, struggling a bit under its weight. She looked up to see Jamie stand and knew he'd been speaking to her but all that had registered was the one word that had haunted her dreams for a past year, *"Chère."*

Suddenly it was like she was an observer, watching herself from the outside. Somewhere in the back of her mind, she realized that she'd frozen in place and dropped the tray to the floor, shattering the serving dishes and sending food in all directions. But it was as if she was watching the events unfold as an observer, everything happening to someone else.

Bree felt people surrounding her and heard the sound of voices, but they sounded so distant she wasn't able to make out their words over the roaring in her ears. She had no idea how she'd gotten from the dining room into an office where she now found herself sitting on Jamie's lap. He was so tall, even cradled in his care, her head easily fit under his chin. She felt like a child, small and fragile but safe.

Feeling the small prick of a needle in her arm, she looked up to see Zach Lamont's concern and knew he'd spoken to her, but she had no idea what he'd said. Bree tried to re-engage, suddenly realizing she'd done it again. *Damn, I haven't had a full-blown panic attack in months, I thought I was past it, these people must think I'm a lunatic.*

Oddly, it was Kat's voice that finally made it through

the fog.

"I know that look, girlfriend, and no, we do not think you're nuts. You just knock that shit off right now and come back to us, you hear me?"

"Katarina, language." Bree recognized that voice, it belonged to Alex Lamont. She was finally beginning to swim to the surface, slowing making her way through a dense haze clouding her mind. It was like trying to maneuver through Jell-O—God, she hated how difficult it was to push herself through that nonsense. Her counselor had made the analogy and for some reason, it had seemed bizarrely perfect.

Looking up into Jamie's face she saw how worried he was, she finally managed to lick her lips to force out the words.

"You called me *Chère*. It's really you, isn't it? You're my Cajun Angel, aren't you?" She saw his stunned expression and the confusion in his eyes. "You rescued me. You carried me out of hell… and you called me *Chère*."

JAMIE'S HEART HAD nearly stopped when he'd seen the stricken look on Bree's face just before she'd dropped the tray. Then she'd fallen ass over tea kettle, as his mama had always said, into what appeared to have been a full-blown flashback. He was sure she hadn't been cognizant enough to realize he'd scooped her up in his arms and carried her out of the chaos that had followed the explosion of food and china when the heavy tray hit the floor.

Zach Lamont had been the medic for their Special Forces team and had snagged his med bag from the small closet in their office. When they hadn't been able to bring her back from what was clearly a dangerous psychological ledge, he'd suggested they administer a mild sedative. Jamie and Alex had both nodded their approval, and Alex had stilled Ethan when he'd started to voice a protest.

As Alex spoke in soft tones to Ethan off to the side, Jamie was only able to catch a few of the words, but enough to know Catherine had warned them this might occur, so the Lamont brothers hadn't been as surprised as everyone else by Bree's reaction.

When his little blonde beauty finally started to come back to the present, Jamie was completely leveled by her words. Bree Hart was Sabrina Gillette? A part of him was shocked to his core, but on another level, it made perfect sense. It explained why she'd seemed so familiar, and why he'd felt such a deep connection to her.

Hell, it even explained the sense both he and Jantz had shared that she was either a spook or in some kind of witness protection program. Perfect backgrounds are almost always created, and when Mitch Grayson had shared the details of hers with them, they had both started watching for any signs of deception indicating she used Catherine Lamont as a way into ShadowDance. They hadn't seen a shred of evidence she was anything but sincere, so the next logical conclusion was she was under the protection of some alphabet agency. Now he found himself biting back his anger because it was glaringly obvious that agency wasn't doing jack shit to help her.

"Oh, *Chère*, I can hardly believe that it's you." Jamie lifted his palms and placed them gently on both sides of her face, his thumbs stroking her cheeks with feather softness. He had to stop and take several deep breaths to maintain his composure. "They told me you'd died from the injuries you had sustained. How could they make such a mistake? How did that happen? Where have you been? How did you end up here?" When he noticed hesitance flash in her eyes, he added, "I need to know, sweetness. I want to know just who to thank for the fact you are now safely nestled in my arms. I want you to know, I'm not letting you go so easily this time, *Chère.*"

Ethan moved to his side and pulled one of her trembling hands into his own. Jamie kept her securely in his arms as he slowly turned her so they all three faced Alex and Zach Lamont who had taken up their usual positions on either side of the fireplace mantel.

The natural rock fireplace took up the largest part of one wall in the brothers' massive office. Two walls were floor-to-ceiling windows, one set looking out over the drive leading to the mansion and The Club's entrance. The other windows faced the gardens and back deck. When Katarina had been injured twice in their home, the brothers had replaced all the windows in the mansion with bulletproof glass and installed a security system that rivaled Fort Knox.

Smiling to himself, Jamie was pleased to know that Bree was safely ensconced behind those same protections. It was obvious if she'd had to give up her former life and change her identity, there was an ongoing threat. Added to the fact Catherine Lamont evidently felt Bree continued to be in some kind of serious danger and that realization sent shards of icy-cold fear through Jamie's heart.

Ethan was gently tracing invisible circles on her shaking palm, but Jamie knew the move would begin to calm her soon. The palms were particularly sensitive to small bits of massage therapy, and Jamie was grateful his friend had thought to use it. Katarina Lamont moved to speak with Alex, and Jamie watched as one of the most Dominant men he'd ever known looked down at his tiny spitfire of a wife with nothing but tenderness.

Both Jamie and Ethan had been on the same team with Alex and Zach. Had you told either of them Alex Lamont would be completely taken with a diminutive woman who expertly led both of her husbands to believe themselves to be in charge, they'd both have laughed you into obscurity.

Seeing Alex and Zach with Kat had been eye-opening for several of their teammates. Most of them would readily admit to being envious of the love their friends had found. Jamie knew he and Ethan had recently talked extensively about finding their own woman and settling down. It warmed Jamie's heart to know he and Ethan agreed the woman curled in his lap was the one they'd been waiting for.

Jamie had a new appreciation for the tenderness he saw in Alex's expression as he trailed the back of his knuckles down Kat's cheek before he turned her toward his brother. Alex then faced the three of them.

"Our sweet wife has suggested that we all return to the dining room and finish our meal before we discuss this situation. I think she has a valid point, her hope is Bree will settle a bit and with the medication Zach administered, Bree is going to need to eat quickly so the 'horse dose' Katarina believes her new friend was given doesn't 'flatten her.'" They all chuckled when Kat received a swat on her lush ass from Zach.

"Kitten, I did not give her a large dose, and you are going to pay for those remarks later." Zach's harsh tone was softened by his smile and the tender kiss he placed on the end of Kat's nose. "I do agree, though, food would be in Bree's best interest. Let's eat, then reconvene here with the rest of the team. Colt and Jenna are planning to join us for dinner, aren't they? I'll call Dylan and Mia to see if they can make it in time for dessert."

Moving back to the dining room, Bree's face turned bright red when the room went silent when they entered. Kat stepped in front of her and gave Bree a fast hug before pulling back and speaking directly to her.

"They are friends, Bree, they are just worried about you. Please don't be embarrassed. We take care of each other, we are family. Now come on, I'm starving, and I don't get to eat until you eat." Kat smiled again and then grinned. "So, you, girlfriend need to just suck it up and sit down, so I can eat my dinner and enjoy my husbands' hands on me when they think you all aren't watching them make me come during dinner."

"Katarina, I swear, you would pull a lion's tail just for the entertainment of the chase. Sit down. Now!" Alex's sharp words made Kat grin even bigger, then with a wink to Bree, she quickly moved to her seat. As they walked by her, Jamie leaned down and whispered his thanks to Kat. She had, with a few simple words, defused a situation that could have easily sent Bree back into meltdown. God, you had to love her.

Kat, you just earned yourself one "Get out of jail free" card.

Chapter 10

BREE FELT SOMEWHAT lethargic from the sedative Zach had given her, but she still managed to thoroughly enjoy the pandemonium the Lamonts referred to as dinner. Sitting between Jamie and Ethan, she noticed at least one of them kept a hand on her at all times. They'd quickly reminded her how they expected her to sit, and Bree found an odd sort of comfort in the fact that they were still doing the things they had said they would do.

In some weird way, it was as if they hadn't all just discovered she was not who they'd been told she was, and Jamie had been the hero who'd pulled her out of hell. Shaking her head at the irony of it all, she felt Jamie lean over and brush his lips up the side of her neck.

"*Mon Chère*," he whispered, "what are you thinking about? And I caution you, tell me the truth, I don't want to have to punish you during your first meal with us."

Bree looked up into his eyes and was immediately lost in their intensity and color. *How will I ever be able to have any secrets from these men? They see my soul.* She had taken so long to answer, Jamie leaned forward and nipped her earlobe, bringing her back to the question he'd asked.

"Um, I was just thinking how much I appreciated that you were both still touching me. That you, well, you seem like… maybe, you are still interested in helping me learn about this lifestyle." She sighed and stiffened, hoping Jamie wouldn't know she was holding back something, but he wasn't fooled.

"And? Out with it all, sweetness. We'll have no secrets, understand? For the record, that includes the colored contacts, baby."

Pickle fudge, I should have known it was too much to ask for that I could retain a sliver of my dignity.

Bree knew she stuttered her answer, "Y–y–yes, Sir. Well, I was just thinking it's as if I get lost in your eyes, and I know you can see clear into my soul. It's a bit unnerving, you know?"

Jamie watched her for so long that she started to fidget, and she finally shifted her focus to her hands as she rolled a small section of fabric between her fingers. Just when she thought she might wear a hole in the semitransparent dress, Jamie grasped her fingers in his own and slowly pried the fabric from them before flattening her palms on her spread thighs. When she looked up, she saw Ethan watching them intently, and she wanted to groan because she was sure he'd heard the entire conversation. *Yep, my humiliation is now complete.*

SITTING IN THE Lamonts' office, Bree glanced around the room and was astonished to see how many people had filtered through the double doors before sitting inside. She noticed the only other woman in the room was the pregnant woman they had introduced as Mia Marshall. Ethan had explained Mia and her husband were both former DEA agents, and Dylan Marshall was now the

Climax County Sheriff. Bree had wanted to hide behind Ethan when they'd been introduced, the man was huge. Remarkably, the minute the mammoth Sheriff smiled, his whole demeanor changed, and watching him dote on his wife won Bree over in a matter of minutes.

Alex stepped forward and spoke to her first. "Bree, I see you have noticed there are quite a number of people in this room. I'm guessing there are more than you had expected. I also want you to notice Katarina and Jenna were not allowed in since they do not have the appropriate clearance levels for this conversation. Rest assured, everyone here has or recently had a clearance level far above whoever you are working with in your protection program." She watched as he visibly stiffened, then added, "And I use the term 'protection' loosely because it took Grayson about ten minutes to find out your identity was created and another thirty minutes until he had your real name."

Bree's gaze snapped to the man who had been introduced to her earlier as Mitch when he stepped forward and laid a file folder on the sofa table in front of her. Sitting down, Mitch spoke directly to her, and even though she could tell he was a Dom, there seemed to be an underlying compassion in his look and voice.

"Bree, this is everything from several agencies that have or are still tracking you as well as a fairly extensive dossier on your parents."

She knew he had to have heard her gasp. It was humbling how quickly they'd been able to gather information she'd been assured was secure. He refocused her attention when he took her hands in his own before continuing.

"Did you know they put a tracking device in you?" It felt like her entire body had suddenly been encased in ice. She started trembling and shaking her head; even she didn't know if it was in denial or in answer to the question. "It's just under the skin on the back of your right shoulder. Do you experience a tingling sensation in that area?"

Stunned that he would know about the tingling she regularly experienced, she nodded then said, "Yes, how did you know about that? Is it in my medical records? The doctors said it was the consequence of some minor nerve damage stemming from the beatings." When her mind finally caught up, she looked frantically from Mitch to Alex and Zach before turning her gaze to Jamie and Ethan—she needed the reassurance she found in their strength.

"Wait! Did he say a tracking device? Do you mean they know where I am at all times? Oh my God, don't they have to get my permission to do that?" She felt just like she had the first time she'd been seasick, but this time, it was as if she'd just been tossed overboard.

Damn, I didn't even know I was still on the flippin' boat, and now, I'm fighting the waves—again. When is this nightmare ever going to end?

Mitch held on to her hand when she'd tried to pull back. "Stay with me here, Bree, we knew about the device when you came through the front gate. We have very sophisticated detection equipment, and we've been jamming the signal since you got here, but that doesn't mean they don't know where you are. They would have had you until you passed through the main gate." He gave her hand a squeeze before he placed it in Ethan's outstretched one before he stood and moved back.

Bree felt like she had fallen through Alice's looking glass again, and suddenly, the room felt very hot and things started to spin. She startled when Mitch Grayson was instantly back kneeling in front of her speaking in soft tones.

"Breathe with me, sweetie, come on, let's slow it down." He gently turned her, so she was facing Ethan, and she started to panic.

"No! Focus on making your breathing match mine." She felt Ethan put her hand on his chest. He was giving her a point of focus, and she recognized it was his voice that replaced Mitch's.

ALEX LAMONT WATCHED as Ethan and Jamie worked to get Bree settled. He hadn't read the entire report yet, but what he read had turned his stomach. The small woman in front of him had endured things no human should ever experience. To have it happen to any woman was enough to make him insane, and he could see by the strained looks on the other men's faces around the room each of them was right there with him.

Mia Marshall had been sitting off to the side, thumbing through a copy of the file when he saw her freeze and look up to her husband and silently signal for him to look at what she'd found. Alex walked to where they stood, looking down at the names of several Middle Eastern terrorist organizations they had dealt with since leaving the Special Forces. He had known her parents weren't the missionaries they'd pretended to be, but he was surprised they were involved at this level.

He and Zach had put together a crack team of former operatives who worked as private contractors for various governments. They'd run across these names more than once, and in his mind, the game had just shifted from Little League to the World Series. These people were not easily dispatched, hell, Uncle Sam had been tracking most of these individuals for several years.

Alex loved that they could pick and choose their missions. The business was lucrative and perfect for the adrenaline junkies most of them freely admitted being. Each member of their team was involved in deciding which assignments they would take on and which ones to walk away from because they were nothing more than suicide missions. Every member of their team considered their change of employment a win-win situation. The names of the men and organizations listed in the file were all on all of Uncle Sam's watch lists and for a moment, he wondered exactly who Bree Hart/Sabrina Gillette might be bringing to their door. Zach had stepped up alongside him and voiced the question they'd all been thinking but hadn't spoken aloud.

"Why? Why would they go after a small-time doctor who was working in remote clinics around the Congo? How'd she manage to land on their radar? And why is our government tracking her?"

Mitch Grayson was their computer and communications specialist and had put the file together in a matter of hours. When he moved into their circle, he nodded to the door as Ethan and Jamie made their way out of the room with Bree between them.

"They're taking her upstairs, she really doesn't have any information to share. From what I've learned, she was targeted because of her parents, but that's a long story. I can tell you she didn't know anything about what her parents were involved in and hasn't been in contact with them since learning about their numerous deceptions. I've got a call into Doc, he'll be here in the morning. For tonight, Ethan and Jamie will be able to distract her, I think." He smiled and they all shared a chuckle, knowing just how the two Doms would distract the beauty they had so obviously claimed as their own.

Chapter 11

Bree didn't remember walking back up the stairs to her room but she did remember feeling the strength and anger radiating off both Ethan and Jamie, yet she somehow understood their frustration wasn't directed at her. Just as they closed and locked the door, she turned to them and with a conviction she was sure surprised them.

"Take it out. Take it out right now." When both men gaped at her in astonishment she added, "I can't do it myself because of where it is. But I can direct you. Do you have a medical kit? I know Catherine said one of her sons was a medic in the Special Forces… that's probably the one who gave me the shot. That was Zach, right? Maybe he has what you need. Can you please get that kit? I'll make sure it has everything we'll need." When neither one moved, she put her hands on her hips and gave them a questioning look.

Ethan seemed to recover first, he'd taken in her, *Why aren't you moving?* stance before he looked at Jamie and grinned.

"Welcome back, Bree. Now, why don't you tell us what Sabrina Gillette did in the Congo? Personally, I'm guessing it was medical, what do you think, Master Jamie?"

She knew he had deliberately used the title of Master just to set the tone. She might be a submissive, but she wasn't an idiot.

"Sabrina Gillette was a physician, a pediatrician to be specific, but she treated all ages because she didn't have the backbone to say no to anyone needing help." Bree felt the tears fill her eyes before she added, "Sabrina loved practicing medicine. It was all she had ever wanted to do, and she feels lost without it. She entered college early—very early, not because she was particularly gifted. No, it was more she studied all the time because there was nothing else to do in all those remote locations."

Bree knew it sounded odd speaking about herself in the third person, but it really was how she felt. It was as if she'd been a whole other person before she'd been captured and tortured by terrorists who assumed she knew all about her parents' *real* occupation. Frack! She hadn't planned to tell these men so much and damned well hadn't wanted to cry. Her parents had drilled it into her as long as she could remember, *"Crying is for babies and weaklings. Gillettes are neither of those things."*

She had never understood how missionaries could be so cold and demanding of their only child, but she sure understood it now. They hadn't been the evangelical angels she'd always considered them to be. Once she'd learned they were actually agents who had worked undercover her entire life, things had started to fall into place. Of course, by the time she'd been given all of this valuable information, she'd already endured unimaginable torture at the hands of a band of lunatics who refused to believe she wasn't either directly involved or at least harboring information about the activities of the people she had only known as devoted servants of God.

They had tried to convince her, but she had refused to take the word of the men who had held her captive. She'd been so sure they'd mistaken her family for another. It wasn't until she was recovering in a military hospital that she'd learned the truth.

Oh yeah, you're a freaking child genius alright... all those years and all those clues and did you flipping figure it out? Christ Almighty, did you even question it? Hell, no! What an idiot!

A sharp slap to her right ass cheek brought Bree's attention back to the men standing in front of her. Ethan's expression reminded her of those cartoon characters whose face goes red and steam whistles out of their ears while Jamie's beautiful Caribbean-blue eyes had turned a stormy gray that reminded her of the Atlantic Ocean during hurricane season. Without thinking she spat out, "Hey, what was that for?" She was rubbing her hand over her stinging ass and glaring at them both. Jamie grabbed her wrist before she even saw him move.

"Keep your hands at your sides. That swat was to bring you back to us. Where did you go? And I'll remind you yet again to answer honestly. We *will* punish you for lying, and we *will* know, I promise you that."

Bree was edging toward pissed off but managed to rein in most of the snark before she said, "Well, I was just thinking about everything that's happened over the past year, and sometimes, those memories are a bit overwhelming as I'm sure you can imagine. Now, are you going for that med kit, or do I need to do it myself?"

She felt herself slipping back into doctor mode and damn if that didn't feel just about forty-two shades of fine. She'd missed practicing medicine more than she had ever thought possible. Oh, for sure they could keep the long hours and rotten conditions, but helping people in need was just about the most perfect job in the entire world, and she couldn't imagine doing anything else.

Ethan took a step forward and was so close, she could feel his body heat through the dress they'd given her to wear. Well, if you really wanted to call the wisp of fabric just this side of transparent and held together by a bit of decorative cord just above her breasts a dress. When she started to take a step back, it sounded as if he growled and she froze.

"Don't you dare move." She wondered what she'd done to make them so angry, but then she remembered they were supposed to be teaching her how to be a sub and apparently, they didn't appreciate her *zoning out* during class, so to speak.

Quickly deciding that perhaps she needed to do some damage control, she dropped her gaze to the floor and whispered, "I'm sorry, Sirs. I get lost in the memories and space out sometimes. The counselors said it will get better... eventually. I try to not let everything swamp me... but to be honest, I'm freaking out about having that thing inside me." She shuddered but went on, "I should probably just move on. I'm worried about bringing trouble here. Damn it, there are children living in this house. Catherine Lamont's my friend, and you are all her family and friends. If anything happened to any of you, I'd never forgive myself." She felt the trembling begin deep inside herself but was powerless to suppress it. "I'd like to get the device out before I leave though. If you'll get the kit, I'm sure we can make a small incision and remove it... Please, will you help me do that?"

Ethan stepped forward and placed his hands on either side of her face, using his thumbs to wipe away tears she hadn't even realized were falling.

"No, Love, not just now. I know you are upset about the chip, but taking it out tonight is not an option. We'll have Doc Woods come up tomorrow, and he and Zach can remove it. We'll keep you here, so our jamming equipment is effective. We don't want the device destroyed." She looked at him questioningly, and he smiled. "We'll play with whoever is tracking you a bit before we snatch them up."

ETHAN WATCHED BREE'S expression as it became a bit unfocused when Jamie moved behind her and smoothed his hands around her upper arms to cup her breasts. He gently rolled her beaded nipples between his thumb and middle finger until they were tight peaks.

"Besides, we want to play with you tonight and if you are hurt or groggy from meds, we can't, *Chère*." Jamie whispered against the sensitive shell of her ear.

Ethan relaxed as he watched Bree lean her head back until it rested on Jamie's chest. Her face flushed when she realized she'd actually moaned out loud.

Reaching forward, Ethan swept his fingers under the straps of Bree's dress slowly moving them to the side until they drifted off her small shoulders. He watched the fabric float to the floor like a gentle breeze. He deliberately let his gaze sweep down her body in a sensual visual caress before bringing his eyes back up to meet hers.

"You are stunning. You quite simply take my breath away, love." He slowly traced her delectable curves with his hands and watched her shiver as chill bumps raced over her lightly tanned skin. She was so responsive to his touch and watching her eyes dilate with her arousal was all the encouragement he needed to continue.

For the first time since he had discovered the joys of dominance in the bedroom, Ethan felt as if he was auditioning. There wasn't any other way to describe the insecurity moving through him as he took in the gorgeous woman standing before him completely bare to his gaze. When he looked over her head at Creed, Ethan could tell his friend was trying to get his feet under him again as well. She had scars which he assumed she'd gotten at the hands of the crazies who'd captured her, but those marks didn't detract from her ethereal appearance.

Moving his hands down her rib cage, Ethan knelt on one knee and pressed a kiss to her flat belly. Speaking as much to himself as to her, he said, "You are too thin, Love. We'll have to see what we can do about that." He felt her stiffen and guessed she probably already felt she was too heavy. It never ceased to amaze him how many women were under the mistaken impression all men preferred stick figures to real women with real curves.

"I know you don't believe me now, but you will soon. Both of your Masters love the curves that are the hallmark of a real woman. We want to be able to feel all the softness you have to offer and to be able to make passionate love to you without fear of breaking you." Hell, he loved wedging his broad shoulders between a woman's thighs knowing he'd spread her legs wide apart. There wasn't as much joy nestling between two sticks.

Jamie wrapped his arms around Bree, and Ethan smiled to himself at this friend's subtle monitoring of her every reaction, cataloging each muscle twitch and change in respiration. They always used their different styles as Doms to bring the maximum pleasure to the woman between them.

Over the years, Ethan had often wondered if the Cajun-French lothario could bring a woman to orgasm by simply talking to her—the man definitely had a way with words. Flicking his gaze upward, he saw Bree lean back into Creed, her eyes half-lidded with lust as she let their touch light her skin on fire. Ethan gave Jamie a quick signal he knew Bree wouldn't catch, telling him it was time to begin. The flush of her skin and the trembling of her muscles was a "go" signal for them to move ahead.

Ethan watched as Jamie steadily increased the pressure on Bree's tightly peaked nipples as he rolled the stiff tips between his fingers. He watched silently as Jamie leaned forward and speak so close to her ear the wisps of his breath teased the sensitive flesh along her hairline.

"You are a dream come true in so many, many ways. I have wished a thousand times I'd had one more chance to look into your beautiful eyes before I watched them wheel you away. I spoke to you in my dreams and prayed the angels had welcomed you home when I was told you hadn't survived. I saw their color in a thousand different objects but none of it mattered because you were gone." They both felt the shiver that raced through her before Jamie continued what could only be described as verbal seduction.

"I was convinced God had turned his back on me because of the enormous karma debt soldiers incur. But now? Now I know my *grand-mère* was right, and God's infinite capacity for forgiveness is surpassed only by his grace in giving us things we don't really deserve because that is the only way I can explain him giving me a second chance with you."

Ethan was thrilled to feel Bree tilt her pelvis forward and then back again, so her ass pressed closer to Jamie's erection. Even though the temptation was nearly too much to resist, he was overjoyed her body's natural responses were kicking in. When she'd admitted earlier she had no real previous sexual experience, he'd worried she would have trouble responding to the typical Ds triggers.

He was thrilled to see that her body seemed to know exactly what it needed even if her mind was having trouble keeping up. Ethan knew Jamie was slipping dangerously closer to the role of lover than Dom, the man continually skating a serpentine pattern over the line. Ethan was grateful when his friend recognized the need for him to step in. Watching as Jamie nuzzled her ear, running his tongue around the outside of its tender shell before whispering, "*Chère*, you are an answered prayer and I can't wait to show you all the ways we can enjoy one another."

When Jamie stepped back, Ethan pressed forward, closing the small space between himself and the dazed beauty standing so close, he could feel the heat of her body through his clothes. He wanted to shout for joy when Bree leaned toward him as if drawn by some unseen force. Her willingness to accept them both equally from the beginning was beyond anything he'd ever have hoped to find in any woman.

Most of the women they had shared had seemed to crave the dominance, but it often seemed they preferred playing with Creed, merely tolerated him because they recognized the two men as the package deal they were. The fact Bree responded to them both equally was another reason to believe they'd finally found the woman they could spend the rest of their lives loving.

Running his hands over her shoulders, then trailing them slowly down her arms, he encircled her tiny wrists in his large hands and slowly moved them together and held them at the small of her back. Grasping them both with one hand, essentially binding them, he felt her begin to shake. Before she could tumble into fear, he leaned forward and sucked a peaked nipple into his mouth. Using his tongue to press the tender flesh against the roof of his mouth before slowly moving toward her other breast, he spoke against her heated flesh.

"I want you to know how pleased we are that you are letting your body speak for you, love. The way your breasts are all but reaching out for my attention when your arms are behind your back is beautiful. And the fact that you have given me your trust by letting me hold you in this position is an amazing gift indeed."

Ethan knew he was playing a bit outside the regular parameters of a Ds scene, but the importance of easing their frightened little sub into their world overrode any concern he had for following protocol. When he felt her breathing become little more than small panting breaths, he used his tongue to paint slow circles around her other nipple and blew a small puff of air on the damp skin, watching as it drew up into an even tighter bud. Speaking to her again, he started letting the steel return to his voice.

"Bree, I want you to spread your legs apart. Make sure your feet are a bit more than shoulder width and turn your feet slightly to the outside." He watched as she quickly moved to get into position, doing exactly as he'd asked. He could tell she felt slightly unbalanced by the position, but she didn't shift to make herself more comfortable. Ethan saw Jamie step up behind her again and was glad to know the sweet woman in front of him would be able to just let herself float in the sensations without worrying she was going to fall over backward. He'd known when he'd given her the instructions it would be an uncomfortable pose and he was thrilled she'd trusted they wouldn't let her fall. He'd learned years ago trust was built one small step at a time and was grateful Bree's ability to trust hadn't been completely decimated by all she had endured.

Leaning forward and placing soft kisses on each of her eyelids, he said, "We weren't going to make sweet love to you tonight, Pet. We didn't think you were ready for that yet, but I believe we need to rethink that assessment. Believe me when I tell you, this change suits us both because there is not anything Master Jamie and I want more than to sink our aching cocks deep inside your sweet body. We intend to give you the release your body and soul are both crying out for. Would you like that, Love?"

Chapter 12

BREE FELT LIKE she was going to explode from need alone. She couldn't fathom how she was going to survive an orgasm at these men's hands. Weren't people supposed to be *actually having sex* when they came? *Geez, you'd think a doctor would know this stuff.*

The only thing she knew right at this moment was that her brain wasn't firing on all its cylinders, and she didn't care. She was starting to worry she would well and truly die of embarrassment if, later, she found out that this was the ultimate *newbie* mistake. Just as she was starting to really work herself into "a state" as her mother used to say, she felt a sharp slap on the inside of her thigh and looked down to see Ethan frowning at her.

"Stop worrying yourself about every little detail. Your job is to feel—nothing else, is that clear?"

Bree could tell Ethan was frustrated with her, but not because she was inexperienced. No, she was sure his frustration was because she wasn't staying "present." Vowing to rein in her fleeting thoughts and insecurities, she nodded her head. Before her head had even stopped moving, she remembered Jamie telling her that she'd be expected to speak her answers, so she quickly added, "Yes, sir, I understand."

"Very good. Now, let's see if we can get your body

back on track for that release it needs so badly before we slide deep into this sweet pussy, shall we?" He'd no sooner spoken the words than he leaned forward and spread her soaking folds apart with his fingers. A second later, Ethan covered her throbbing clitoris with his mouth and sucked.

Bree was convinced, between one heartbeat and the next, someone had strapped her to the side of a rocket and launched her into deep space. She'd barely registered her body starting to tremble and Jamie's arms tightening around her when she heard a scream pierce the silence around her, and everything around her erupted into a kaleidoscope of brilliant colors racing past her as if she'd been dropped into a vortex of swirling, melted crayons.

It was several long moments before she realized what she had heard was actually her own scream of release as she'd fallen over into a soul-shattering orgasm, and the rushing sound she thought was wind from her drop through the colorful tunnels had actually been the sound of the blood roaring through her ears.

Holy crap on a cricket, all those books I've read were right. If an orgasm feels that good without sex, I'm not sure I'll live through one that involves their cocks inside my pussy... but I'm damn anxious to try.

ETHAN HAD NEVER been as thrilled with a sub's response as he was with Bree's. She'd flooded his tongue with her sweet honey and he'd been happy to savor every drop. Jesus, Joseph, and sweet Mother Mary, Bree tasted like pure sugar and sunshine. Thank God Creed had been ready, his arm banded securely around her narrow waist because Ethan wasn't sure if she would have collapsed or launched herself skyward.

She was so fucking perfect he worried for just a moment that it was all too good to be true. When he looked up at her sated expression and rapidly drooping eyelids, he was able to bring himself back to the moment and refocus on the remarkable woman in front of him. Standing up he cupped her sweet face in his hands.

"You are a treasure, and I want you to know how pleased your Masters are with you, Love. Now, let's get you up on the bed. I know you are physically exhausted. Master Jamie and I want you to start taking better care of yourself. As a matter of fact, we're going to insist on it, but right now, we're going both going to slide in deep and let you feel just how desirable you are." Nodding to Jamie, he stepped back and watched as his friend lowered himself over Bree and slid his sheathed cock slowly into her pussy.

"Oh my God, *Chère*, you feel fantastic. The walls of your sweet pussy are flexing around my cock and taunting my control. You may well push me past my ability to hold myself back, and that is not how I want this to go." Ethan could hear Jamie taking slow, deep breaths and knew he was desperately trying to bring his body back under his mind's control—no easy task from the tortured look on his face.

Jamie began slowly sliding in and out of her channel, watching as her expression changed from startled by the new sensations to heated lust tinged with pure desire. The metamorphosis was one of the most beautiful things Ethan could remember ever having the privilege to see. Watching Bree's eyes widen as she approached another climax was pure eroticism.

The first release had blindsided her, but she was definitely going to feel this one coming. Ethan could hardly wait to begin teaching her to delay her orgasms, so they were more intense. It was often one of the hardest things for submissives to learn, but certainly, one that paid off in spades. Listening to her soft pleas, he leaned down and whispered in her ear.

"Master Jamie is waiting for you to go over first, Love. Come for him, *now*."

Ethan knew her body had responded before her mind had time to process the words because her scream had been instantaneous. Jamie's shout followed right on the heels of hers and watching them made Ethan so hard, he wasn't sure he was going to last long enough to give her body the attention it deserved.

After Jamie moved to her side, they spent long minutes touching her with tender caresses, letting her know exactly how important her gift had been.

"Are you sore? If you are, please tell me, and I'll wait to make love to you. I want you to enjoy the experience and look back on it with fondness." Seeing a flash of relief in her eyes, Ethan wondered how long it had been since anyone besides Catherine Lamont had taken a genuine interest in the welfare of the beautiful woman lying next to him.

"I am a little sore, but I want you, too… and I don't want you to feel otherwise. I want you to make love to me. Could we just go slow?"

His heart was lost for a moment—shocked she would put his need above her own comfort. There was an inherent sweetness in her, but there the fire of desire was rekindling as well.

"Oh, sweet one, I want you, too, more than you know. I'll go just as slow as I can, but your body calls to mine in a way that tempts my control. So, if you get uncomfortable, tell me and we'll figure out something else, alright?" She smiled and nodded her head as enthusiastic as she had been the first time. *Christ, she is amazing.*

He rolled onto his back and smiled at her puzzled expression. "I'm going to give you a measure of control this time, sweet sub. Let Master Jamie help you mount up."

Jamie lifted her effortlessly, helping her get into position. It was a good thing Jamie kept a hand on her because Ethan had been so lost in the moment. God in heaven, he hadn't been ready when she positioned his tip at her entrance, and in a move so quick, Ethan didn't have time to prepare for the tsunami of sensation when she dropped suddenly, fully seating him inside her. Her tissues felt sweetly swollen from their attention, making her tighter than he'd been prepared for, and he sucked in several deep breaths trying to slow his raging libido.

"Oh, sweet Jesus, you feel so incredible. I have no idea how Master Jamie maintained any control at all." Wrapping his hands around her slender hips, he held her tight. "Stay still for a few seconds, Love." He could feel her flexing muscles and might have chalked it up to involuntary contractions if he hadn't seen a fleeting grin before her head rolled back, and she seemed to lose herself in a move so blatantly erotic his breath caught. "Okay, you little minx, I saw that grin, you are deliberately tempting me, so I know you are ready. I want you to set a pace that suits you, but I'll control the angle of penetration, do you understand?"

"Yes, I understand... Sir." He watched as she positioned her feet under her so that she was essentially doing squats over him and the feeling of her body sliding up and down over his shaft was intoxicating.

"Oh fuck, that is so good. You are going to be the death of me, no questions about it." He let her stroke him several more times before he tilted his hips forward just enough he knew the tip of his cock would move over her sweet spot with every pass. Her gasp told him his angle had been perfect, and he relished the sound of her panting breaths and soft moans.

He was at the end of his own control, so he canted his hips just a bit further, and on the next stroke, he felt her go completely liquid around him just before she shouted, "Oh please, I have to... I need to... *please*."

Ethan didn't have time for his usual questions about what she wanted, hell, he'd been proud of himself for holding off long enough to shout, "Come," before they both exploded in an orgasm that literally had him seeing small pinpoints of light dancing in his vision. She collapsed onto his chest, and he cherished the feeling of her breasts pressing against him. When they finally caught their breath, he realized his cock was still inside her. Knowing he needed to dispose of the used condom, he reluctantly helped Jamie lift her to the side.

After disposing of the condom, he returned to find Jamie sitting in one of the chairs looking into the gardens. Bree was cradled in his arms, her eyes closed and her breathing slow and even. Ethan turned down the bed and watched as his friend laid her gently on the mattress before pulling the covers back into place.

Jamie's expression reflected the satisfaction Ethan felt as her eyelids fluttered open. Once they had her settled and were sure she was drifting back to sleep, he let his words whisper over her.

"We're going to go back downstairs for a few minutes while you rest. We'll secure the door and leave the bedside light on for you. Rest assured, we'll be back soon. We want to hold you while you sleep. Don't leave this suite without one of us. Should you need anything—call us. We've shown you how to operate the intercom—don't hesitate to use it." He kissed her lightly on the tip of her nose before moving aside for Creed.

Watching as Creed leaned down close and whispered words of praise in her ear, Ethan couldn't help but smile at the satisfaction he felt watching them together. Jamie continued to speak to her in French as a wistful smile played over her lips just before she let herself slide over the edge into sleep.

BREE WOKE UP feeling like she was floating on a cloud. Even though she didn't remember exactly where she was or how she'd gotten there, all she wanted was to snuggle further down into the most comfortable bed she'd ever slept on. But before she was able to lose herself back into a luxurious sleep, the events of the past few hours started to make their way to the surface. She knew she had to make her way downstairs and find out what was going on; after all, she was the one ultimately responsible. Damn it, she'd brought trouble to the Lamonts' home. Endangering Catherine's family and friends was the last thing she'd ever wanted to do.

Looking around the suite, Bree didn't see her luggage and thought that was odd since she remembered Alex saying they'd moved her things into the suite. Shrugging it off, she decided to check the drawers in the enormous dresser, hoping to find something decent enough, she could go in search of the powwow she was sure the men were having about her.

Trying to hold her irritation at bay at not being included in the discussions, she remembered how wonderful Jamie and Ethan had made her feel and how she had been more than willing to slide right into sleep. She wasn't sure how long she'd slept, but since they weren't back in the room, she didn't think it could have been that long. When she opened the first drawer, she was shocked to find her own clothing neatly arranged inside.

She easily located a pair of yoga pants and a matching T-shirt, but even though she searched all the other drawers, she couldn't find any panties. At first, she'd thought it was more than a little odd that her underwear was missing, but then she remembered all the romance novels she'd read and sighed.

This explained the twinkle in Zach Lamont's eyes when he and Alex said they'd already moved her into their sister's suite. They'd taken anything they didn't think she would need. Shuddering to think about Alex and Zach Lamont seeing the plain-Jane panties she'd had in her luggage, Bree really wasn't surprised they'd gone missing. Hell, she should probably be grateful.

Sighing to herself, she moved to the bathroom. After freshening up and running a brush through her unruly hair, she left the suite and made her way down the hall. She'd hadn't gone far when she suddenly remembered Ethan's warning to not leave the suite without one of them but decided it was already too late to salvage.

Damn it, she was a grown woman and should be able to move around inside the house without anyone's permission. Just as she neared a staircase, she realized this wasn't the same one they'd come up earlier but figuring it would still lead her to the main floor, she quickly made her way down. Since she was barefoot, she was moving almost silently and fleetingly wondered if anyone was aware she'd left the suite. Remembering all the security monitoring equipment she'd seen outside, she almost laughed out loud. *Oh yeah, you can bet your sweet ass someone somewhere knows that suite door was opened.* When she passed one of the security cameras, she looked directly at it and gave it an innocent finger wave.

Just as she made her way to the bottom of the stairs she heard men's voices, so she moved silently in that direction. Standing outside a door that obviously led into Alex and Zach Lamont's office, Bree was shocked by the discussion taking place inside.

If you'd asked her a few minutes ago, Bree would have sworn there wasn't anything left of her heart for her parents to break, but she'd have been wrong. Hearing one of the men explain her parents and their employers were suspected of hiding highly sensitive information on a chip they'd secretly put inside her body made her eyes fill with bitter tears and a renewed sense of betrayal. How could they be so heartless as to place their only child in so much danger? What went through the minds of people that made them think of others merely as vessels to be used and discarded rather than individuals? It was so far beyond Bree's comprehension—she couldn't imagine how someone's mind had to work for that to be considered acceptable.

JUST AS THEY had reentered the Lamonts' downstairs office,

Jamie heard Mitch describing the various types of chips he thought might have been implanted in Bree's shoulder. Jamie felt a surge of rage move through him the likes of which he'd never experienced before, and by the expression on Jantz's face, he was experiencing the same thing.

Mitch Grayson was a gifted empath, and Jamie was sure he'd pick up on his and Ethan's emotions quickly. As if he'd thought the other man's attention into existence, Mitch turned to them.

"Believe me, I understand your frustration. I've been precisely where you are, so I *get it*. But until we know exactly what we're dealing with, we'll have to keep everything on an even keel so no one outside our inner circle has any idea Bree is anything other than exactly who she presents herself to be. We'll get Doc Woods up here tomorrow to remove the chip, but I'm setting up some precautions just in case it's one of the extreme ones I've been reading about recently." Jamie knew Mitch hadn't missed the confused looks on the faces of his teammates when he continued. "There are several new models out there that are much more sophisticated than the simple GPS models we've seen before."

Alex leaned back in his leather chair, steepling his fingers in front of his chin and said what every person in the room was thinking, "Update us."

Mitch looked around at his teammates and sighed. The tech expert proceeded to explain how the new generation of chips could be downloaded with huge amounts of data and most had batteries capable of lasting for years. The chip itself could also be updated without being removed and replaced. All someone would need was the proper codes and to have the "host" near a wireless device.

Jamie had known Mitch Grayson for years, and there

wasn't a doubt in Jamie's mind the man was holding back something critical. When he couldn't stand it another second Jamie grimaced to himself when he heard the sharp tone of his own voice when he blurted out, "Out with it, Grayson. What are you *not* telling us?" He hadn't meant to be an ass, but his imagination was working at warp speed, and none of his conclusions involved a happily ever after.

Mitch let out a frustrated sigh before continuing, "Some of the devices are set to explode if they are exposed to a sudden temperature change. This means we'll need to be prepared to keep the device very close to Bree's normal body temperature until we can determine exactly what we're dealing with."

Jamie shot to his feet and began pacing, his long stride taking him the length of the room and back in just a few quick steps.

Finally, stopping to look over at Ethan, he said, "We need to be there with her, both of us. I'd rather she didn't know anything about the possibility of the device exploding. Hell, she is already determined to leave because she's worried sick about bringing danger to a place where there are children. She was a pediatrician, for Christ's sake. Even the possibility of being peripherally responsible for harming children is devastating for her."

Jamie looked from Ethan to Colt before finally settling on Alex and Zach. They were all used to deferring to Colt as their former team leader and the current head of their security team and now that the Lamonts were their employers, it was natural to include them when waiting for information and/or assignments.

Shaking his head at his own mental meanderings, Jamie finally looked at Mitch and asked, "So, you're telling me Bree's parents implanted a chip loaded with sensitive data into their only child, so the kidnappers actually had the data at their fingertips all along and didn't know it?"

"Fuck!" Zach Lamont's muttered curse was echoed around the room before Alex raised his hand to still the frustrated murmurs of the others that followed.

"Hold on, let Grayson finish. I want to make sure we have a clear picture of all the possible outcomes before we make any plans." Jamie had always admired Alex's ability to remain calm in the midst of a shit storm, but his growing concern was evident from his tight-sounding words.

Mitch cleared his throat before adding, "I've had her phone since she arrived. We took it out of her car as soon as Creed moved her inside because it was also broadcasting in a big way. They had tags on this girl out the yin-yang. There was also one in each piece of luggage and her purse. Trust me when I say, they don't want to lose track of her. Now, do I think all of these are alerts funneled to the same group of people? Not likely, but I'd say several are linked directly to her parents and whoever they're working for. Also, her phone has been ringing continually, and she has a lot of voicemails. Now, while I'm willing to snatch up her phone because its technology makes it a security threat to us as a group, I'm not willing to invade her privacy to a level where I break into her personal voice mail."

Sighing, Mitch leaned back in his chair and Jamie could see his friend was clearly troubled by all the information he'd had to share about Bree. Shaking his head, Mitch muttered, "Bottom line is, I like her. She's the real deal, guys—totally genuine. Rissa and Kat like her, you guys,"—he pointed in Jamie and Ethan's general direction—"are fucking smitten, and it's about damned time, I might add. And if as if all this isn't enough, I've read her file. She was top in her class in medical school. She is a fantastic pediatrician and..." his voice went soft before he finished, "Well, she is exactly the kind of doctor I'd want taking care of my children."

Alex sat up and looked at Mitch for long seconds before asking, "Cut to the chase, Mitch, how much danger is this young woman in? And how do we help her?"

Mitch's next words were like a gut punch to Jamie.

"A lot. Bree Hart is in danger on at least two fronts and likely more. We're working to back trace each of the devices, and we'll get them all done by midafternoon tomorrow, at the latest. But I can assure you, the greatest threat is from her parents and/or their superiors. I'm convinced there is data on the chip in her shoulder they don't want in the wrong hands, and any hands other than theirs will be considered the enemy. My guess is the kidnappers were waiting on orders from their commanders when your team snatched her out from under them, so they're most likely looking for her as well."

Jamie noticed there was a lot of silent communication taking place between Alex, Zach, and Colt. He'd been a member of their teams long enough to know that meant there was likely more—probably a lot more—to the story. Since he'd also been trained by the very best to be the very best this country had to offer when it came to black ops, Jamie knew exactly when he was best served by waiting it out. Letting his gaze slide to Jantz, Jamie knew those same thoughts were racing through Ethan's mind as well, but he wasn't sure Ethan was going to be able to hold his tongue for long.

Colt Matthews finally took the floor, speaking in what they all called his "Team Leader" voice. "As I'm sure you can imagine, the minute this young woman came on our radar we started working this case, and I'm not talking about when she drove that piece of shit car through the front gate either." Looking directly at Jamie and Ethan he growled, "Get your woman a safe vehicle, gentlemen, the heap she drove up here scares the shit out of me!" Smiling at their nods, he turned back to the rest of the group.

"As soon as Catherine told Alex she wanted to send Bree this way, we got to work, and our sources tell us there are several factions involved in this mess, and depending on the data on the chip, there may be more players than we've anticipated." Turning his gaze to Dylan Marshall, Colt said, "We need your deputies to be particularly diligent about watching for anybody new in town. Likely her parents and their merry little group of banditos will be the first ones to show, but that's just our best guess."

It surprised Jamie when Zach spoke up, saying "Creed... Jantz... we've got her back. I can tell by your expressions you're worried, and I just want to get this out on the table right now. Let those worries go and concentrate on being present for Bree. This woman has endured unimaginable torture and heartbreaking betrayal—she's going to need you in the days to come."

Mitch appeared to be only half tuned in to the conversation as his fingers raced over the keys of the laptop in front of him when Jamie saw him suddenly stiffen and sit up straight. When he cocked his head slightly to one side in what they all recognized as his "listening pose," every person in the room froze. Mitch shook his head, giving them the signal to continue speaking while he moved slowly to the door to the back hallway which wasn't completely closed. Jerking the door open quickly, he reached through, and Jamie heard a startled squeak just before Grayson pulled a very shaken Bree into the room.

Chapter 13

BLINKING RAPIDLY AT the bright lights in the room, Bree stood in stunned silence, taking in the looks on the faces of the men and the lone woman in the room. The woman she remembered was named Mia smiled at her warmly. Her hosts' tight smiles told Bree they were well accustomed to dealing with an unpredictable woman, but it was the stormy looks she was getting from Jamie and Ethan that captured and held her attention.

Jamie moved across the room, quickly reaching her not more than a heartbeat before Ethan flanked her on the other side. Jamie spoke first, "*Chère*, please have a seat before you faint. You are white as a sheet."

Just as Jamie's words registered, Ethan scooped her up and made his way to the small sofa to the side of Alex Lamont's desk. As he settled her on his lap Ethan whispered in her ear, "We'll address your disregard for our instructions when we return to the suite, Love."

The hot zing of arousal shooting through her should have seemed out of place, but it didn't. Instead of scaring her, his warning caused her pussy to flood with wet heat and her nipples to tingle in anticipation.

Catching herself before she moaned aloud Bree tried to recover some semblance of decorum, no easy feat considering she was sitting on Ethan's lap in front of a bunch of former government operatives and agents.

Giving herself a mental slap to refocus on what she'd overheard, she wasn't entirely convinced they were "former" anything. It had sounded an awful lot like they were still very "connected," and she caught herself wondering if perhaps that was why Catherine had been so adamant she would be safe here at ShadowDance.

When she realized the room around her was eerily silent, she looked up into the concerned faces focused on her. Deciding they'd been patiently waiting for her to "reengage," she took a deep breath and let it slowly drain away the tension she'd been holding in.

"I'm sorry, I really hadn't planned to eavesdrop. I got turned around when I left the suite, and when I stepped up to the door, I heard what Mr. Grayson was saying about the chip, and I just froze." Taking several more steadying breaths, she made a concentrated effort to regain control of her racing thoughts, so she could continue.

"I can't tell you how sorry I am for bringing this trouble to your door. I will leave as soon as it's light enough to see. I'm embarrassed to admit I'm scared spitless to drive these roads in the dark." Then with a tension-filled chuckle, she added, "You must all be very skilled drivers to have survived driving here, mercy." She relaxed a bit when she heard soft chuckles around the room. It shouldn't have surprised her that Zach Lamont was the first to move forward and speak.

"Bree, please believe me when I say that while we are very concerned for your safety, we are not overly concerned for the safety of anyone else, including our family because we have complete faith in the abilities of the men in this room to protect them." Then, smiling sweetly at the pregnant woman sitting across the room, he added, "No disrespect intended, Mia, but no one here expects you to be involved except in an advisory capacity, and I'm betting your husband is going to be imposing some mighty stringent guidelines in that regard as well."

When everyone in the room laughed, Bree sensed an immediate shift in the energy and was very grateful Zach had known how close she'd been to making a break for it. Damn it all to frosted donuts, she'd spent her entire life working toward her goal of caring for and treating children as a physician. Even entertaining the thought, she might be endangering the three tykes upstairs or their parents was almost more than she could imagine.

She suddenly realized Zach was still kneeling in front of her and he had taken her hand in his.

"Bree, I know that fight-or-flight look. I can see it in your eyes, sweetness, and I swear if you try to run, I'll personally help your two men paddle your sweet ass. You *are* safe here and here is where you will stay until we are all convinced it's safe for you to go. If you are still of a mind to leave at that time, we won't hold you captive. But sweetness, it's painfully obvious our friends here have staked a claim on you, so I don't figure they'll make it easy for you to go." He chuckled before adding, "If push comes to shove, I'm sure they'll bring out the big guns and sic Kat on you." That brought a roar of laughter from most of the men in the room and before Bree realized what she was doing, she leaned forward and wrapped her arms around Zach's neck and hugged him. When she realized what she'd done, it was too late to do anything but plow ahead so she gave him one last tight squeeze before sitting back and nodding.

"Thank you so much for everything, but especially for your insight and friendship. Your mother's right, you know? This is a very special place, filled with amazing people." She took a deep breath, then met Alex's and Colt's gazes before returning her attention to Zach. "Now, tell me exactly how I can help take down these ass-hats."

JAMIE HAD NEVER been prouder of anyone in his entire life. Bree was obviously way out of her element, terrified, and likely more than a little overwhelmed, but she had just stepped up to the plate and hit it out of the park. When he looked at Ethan, it was obvious his longtime friend was working hard not to be steamrolled by the emotion so clearly written in his expression. Jamie had never seen his longtime friend close to losing his infamous "cool," but at this moment, he seemed to be working very hard to swallow back the same tide of emotion Jamie was trying to hold at bay.

Looking up at Zach, Jamie could only smile when the big man grinned from ear to ear and said, "Good enough. Welcome to the team, Bree." After Zach stood up and moved back to his usual position near the fireplace, they all proceeded to fill Bree in on all the details they'd learned so far. Even though she had very little to add, she was able to provide some dates and locations that might prove valuable.

Just as the meeting was beginning to wind down, Jamie noticed Zach step aside to answer his phone. Noting Zach appeared to be visibly shaken, he started to step forward to ask him what had happened, but Zach stayed him with a quick gesture.

Looking on as Zach conferred with Alex, he noted both

men appeared equally concerned when they approached Bree. Alex Lamont spoke first and even though his voice was pitched low, there was no doubt he was deeply worried.

"Bree, my brother and I have just been told that all three of our children are ill. They are running fevers and have developed an odd rash." Watching Bree's eyes widen, he continued, "Would you mind looking in on them? We have a call into their regular pediatrician and also to Doc Woods but haven't heard from either of them yet. While we hate to impose on you, we are very concerned."

Jamie watched Bree's entire persona shift from the "Warrior Princess" who had just moments before been helping map out a plan of action to "Compassionate Physician," reaching forward to offer a reassuring pat on the arm to a couple of very worried daddies. The change had happened in the blink of an eye—it was the kind of special-effects shift George Lucas lay awake at night trying to mastermind. Bree was immediately on her feet and stepped closer so that she could speak to them both without being overheard.

"Of course, I'll be happy to check on them. I've been anxious to meet them, anyway." Grabbing one of each Alex's and Zach's hands, she added, "I think I know what we're dealing with, but I'll need to examine them to be sure. Please don't worry, because if I'm right, it's really nothing serious. It looks ever so much worse than it actually is."

Chapter 14

BREE BREATHED A huge sigh of relief as soon as she saw the Lamont triplets. Both boys were sporting the bright red cheeks so typical of Fifth Disease and were running low-grade fevers. Little Mary Catherine seemed to be exhibiting the worst symptoms and was also the quietest which worried Bree a bit. When she had explained the children had a fairly common virus that would pass soon enough all three of the parents seemed to relax. Bree picked up Mary Catherine and noted she felt a lot warmer than her brothers, but she didn't want to alarm the little girl's parents, so she tried to subtly take the little girl's temperature. Alex and Zach immediately flanked her, asking questions. Sighing and then chuckling softly, Bree answered all their questions.

"I should have known better than to try to fool a couple of Doms."

As soon as the words left her mouth, Bree regretted speaking out loud because she noticed Ethan and Jamie both stiffen. They had both been standing off to the side, but they'd gone on alert at her attempt at humor. Finally deciding to just ignore them and focus on the baby, Bree asked if it would be alright with Katarina if she gave all three babies a small dose of a non-aspirin pain reliever. She also told her new friends a nice cool bath would help get

Mary Catherine's fever down faster. The minute she mentioned the bath, Alex scooped the baby out of her arms and headed to the nursery's bathroom with Zach hot on his tail.

Kat looked up at Bree and just smiled. "They are just a *bit* overprotective of their little princess. The pain reliever is in the medicine cabinet; if you would write down the dosage after you give it to them, I'll be able to do it through the night. Oh hell, I know full well those two husbands of mine aren't going to let me do this. Would you mind waiting until they are out of there, so you can explain it to them personally? Because sure as a bear shits in the woods, they'll be pounding on your door if they have to get the information secondhand."

"Katarina... Language!" Alex's sharp words were spoken from the bathroom, and Bree nearly laughed out loud at Kat's obvious wince. Alex walked back into the room without the baby, so he could speak with Bree. She'd no sooner explained everything to him than Zach entered with a wet, but much more alert baby snuggled in his arms. Smiling, Bree simply explained everything again, knowing Zach wouldn't be any happier with secondhand information than Alex would have been.

STANDING TO THE side, watching Bree tend to the Lamonts' children had been a great opportunity for both Ethan and Jamie to learn more about the beautiful woman they planned to make their own. She'd handled the children and all three of their parents with grace and compassion that was obviously her true nature.

Bree hadn't hesitated to give the same information multiple times and had all the while kept her hands moving over the children. While the parents had been focused on her words, she had been assessing and reassessing the children's condition until she was satisfied they were going to be fine, then turned to where he and Jamie stood waiting and asked if they were ready to go.

Ethan watched as Jamie stepped forward and simply wrapped his arms around her and spoke close to her ear. When Jamie released her, he had turned her right into Ethan's welcoming embrace.

Ethan hugged her close and whispered, "You are one amazing woman, Bree Hart. This is exactly what you should be doing. The children of this world don't have enough adults who love them and are willing to see to their needs. We need to see what we can do about getting you back to practicing medicine."

As he and Jamie led Bree from the room, he heard Alex and Zach voice their agreement. Alex assured them he would make phone calls first thing in the morning to their contacts in Washington, DC to see what could be done about getting her medical license switched to her new name without it being tagged to her past. Ethan knew perfectly well Mitch Grayson had the computer know-how to hack in and get it done without even breaking a sweat, but he had to admire the Lamont brothers' attempt to do it properly... first.

Chapter 15

AS SOON AS they entered Bree's suite, she felt the energy shift and knew both men were now donning their Dom personas. *I wonder if they stand in front of the mirror and practice that look? Are Doms born or created? Who teaches them how to do all those things to their subs? Someone must provide classes or something because otherwise, there would certainly be a lot of ER visits, and that would get a lot of press. Do you suppose they get a diploma? Would you frame something like that and hang it in your home or office?*

Bree suddenly realized both men were staring at her. *Damn, I did it again. I really have to start staying in the moment. These guys are going to think I'm a flipping loon.* Gasping as she felt a slap on her right ass cheek, she glared up at Ethan.

"Hey! What the hell was that for?"

Ethan's eyes darkened until they looked like black discs and without conscious thought, Bree started to step back but froze at Ethan's sharp, "Don't you dare move." When she looked at Jamie, he looked just as formidable, and she suddenly realized Ethan must have been trying to bring her back from the little mental road trip she'd taken. She could tell they were waiting for her to figure it out or at least to pay attention for more than a few seconds. Deciding she had waited long enough she sighed and spoke to them both.

"Look, it's pretty late, and I'd like to get some rest, so I can check on the babies first thing in the morning before your doctor friend arrives. So, if it's all the same to you, I think I'll say goodnight now." It wasn't that she had really expected her words to work, but she sure hadn't expected the feral grins she saw on the faces of both men.

Jamie was the first to respond. "Oh, *Chère*, I don't think so, but that certainly was a good try, I'll give you that."

She figured they couldn't blame a girl for trying, but she would have been wrong about that as well. Sometimes she just couldn't seem to catch a break. When she realized she was about to slip back into her own little orbit, she made a concentrated effort to focus on what was happening with the two men standing in front of her, studying her like she was the most interesting insect specimen they'd ever seen.

Her head knew she should just stay quiet, but when she was nervous she tended to rattle on and it didn't look like tonight was going to be an exception.

"Well, if you have a problem with me, I suggest you just come straight out with it. We'll sort it through. then you can let me get some sleep. Oh damn, I bet I know. You're miffed because I came downstairs without calling on that intercom thingy, right?"

She would have sworn she heard Ethan growl, and just as she was about to step back, Jamie grabbed her wrist in the enormous mitt he called a hand and pulled her toward a straight-backed chair positioned near the window. She was surprised when he sat down and pulled her to a stop on his right side. He was so tall, even sitting, he was able to look her in the eyes when he spoke.

"You disobeyed a direct order, Bree. That order was in

place for your safety, so *miffed* doesn't quite cover it. We'll be patient while you learn all about the lifestyle we know you are drawn to, and we'll be happy to explain things along the way when they do not relate directly to your safety. Security, as it relates to any woman and particularly *our* woman, will always be our top priority. When you disregard your safety, you will be punished, it's just that simple. Do you understand?"

Bree knew her breathing had become shallow, and she was starting to tremble, but she wasn't sure whether it was from fear of a punishment at Jamie's hand or from excitement about that same punishment. When she nodded her head, his raised eyebrow prompted her to stutter, "Y–yes, I understand." When he continued to stare at her, she quickly added, "Sir."

WHEN THEY HAD first returned to the suite, Jamie hadn't been sure they'd proceed with the punishment Bree had earned by leaving the suite without calling for one of them to accompany her, but she had given them the perfect "in" with her little episode of mentally checking out and her snarky answers. He was sure she had been subconsciously trying to ensure they would stay even though she had tried to dismiss them. He had to fight his smile when she had frozen at Ethan's order to not back away. Holy hell, the woman was such a natural submissive, it was almost as if she'd been tailor-made for him and Ethan.

As he'd pulled her to his side after sitting in the chair, he'd seen her eyes flare with arousal and apprehension when she'd realized what was going to happen. He was deliberately stalling to give her a chance to call a halt to everything, and he also wanted to watch her carefully for any hint of PTSD. He'd witnessed firsthand the results of the intensely brutal beatings she'd been subjected to and wanted to be sure she clearly understood the power of her safe word. He'd made it abundantly clear she was being spanked specifically because she had done something to endanger herself, not because of her connection to her spook parents.

"Bree, your safe word is *red*. You say that word and everything stops. We move away from each other, discuss what went wrong, and how we think it can be prevented in the future. Play stops for that day, period. You are to use your safe word when you are at a point you can no longer tolerate the pain or emotions you are experiencing. Do you understand?"

"Yes, I understand. I say the word *red* and you are done with me." Bree's words were close to what he'd said, but not close enough.

"No, that's not quite right. Let's go over it again because this is probably the single most important element in any Ds relationship and certainly, the most important part of any scene. We will not be *done* with you. We will all simply be finished playing for *that* day. We will take the time we need to evaluate what happened and how we all feel about it." He paused to let her absorb the words.

"Now, all that being said, I want you to know if Master Ethan and I are doing our jobs, we'll be reading your body language and listening to you so closely, you should never have to use your safe word. Also, if we ever think you should have used it and you didn't, you'll get a paddling that will keep you from sitting comfortably for several days." Jamie watched her eyes go wide, and this time, he did let his smile surface briefly and was glad to see her relax a bit.

Ethan stepped forward and explained, "Bree, you'll also have the option of using the word *yellow* if you just want to take a short break, ask a question, or express a concern about the way things are going. We'll encourage you to use this option, particularly in the beginning while you are still learning. This gives you the chance to let us know you are getting close to your 'overload' point. We'll stop and discuss things with you, and we may or may not agree about how to proceed. When you use your 'caution' word, your Masters have the final say about how things proceed. But you can rest assured, each and every decision we make during a scene is governed by what we feel you need. Remember, what you want and what you need are not always one and the same."

Jamie had watched Bree closely for any sign of fear while Ethan had been talking to her and was pleased the only reactions he'd noted had been those associated with arousal. Her nipples were peaked and showing clearly through the thin shirt she wore, and he could smell her sweet juices even through her yoga pants. He could hardly wait to get this punishment out of the way and sink into her sweet pussy. Leaning forward, he tightened his hold on her wrist for just a moment before releasing her and asking her clearly, "Bree, do you want to use your safe word?"

It seemed like forever before she shook her head and quietly said, "No, Sir."

He continued to watch her for several seconds before deciding she really was good to go.

"You are being spanked for disobeying a direct order that was related to your safety. That is a pretty big offense, but since this is all new to you, we'll go fairly easy on you—this time and this time only. You'll be getting ten swats, but we won't require you to count them. Now, pull your pants down to your ankles and lie over my lap." When she grabbed the top of her yoga pants he added, "Do you have on panties, *Chère?*"

"No, sir. Someone stole all my panties." She looked mortified, and Jamie made a mental note to thank Alex and Zach.

"You will always be punished with your ass bare for several reasons, but most importantly, we'll need to see exactly how your skin pinks under our hand. We don't want to do any permanent damage, and it's much easier to monitor how your body is reacting if we can see it."

Jamie had seen her start to tremble when he'd told her to pull down her pants and was pleased she'd let him explain without panicking. When she hooked her thumbs in the elastic and slowly lowered her pants to her ankles, he was sure his throbbing cock was going to spontaneously combust. He was grateful he needed to focus on his next instruction.

"Now lie over my lap and spread your legs. Don't worry, we'll help get you into the proper position."

He'd nearly called the whole thing off when he saw her eyes fill with tears as she draped herself over his lap. The woman was obviously not crying from pain since they hadn't even touched her yet, so he suspected her tears were because she felt she'd disappointed them. He heard her small gasp when he shifted her forward, so her feet were off the floor and her ass peaked and in the perfect position. Ethan moved her legs apart, and when he nodded, Jamie knew her pussy was soaking wet. They'd monitor that closely to make sure the spanking didn't have an adverse effect on her arousal.

Not wanting her to be unnecessarily stressed by anticipation for too long due to her inexperience, he delivered the first several swats in rapid succession. When he slid his hand through her drenched folds after the first four slaps, she moaned and lifted closer into his touch. Jamie looked up and smiled at Ethan who was already grinning like a fool.

Jamie watched as her ivory skin took on a nice deep pink and wanted to prance around the room like a peacock at the sight of his handprints on her bare ass. Nodding to Ethan, he watched as Ethan delivered six strokes that were sharper than his own had been and was sure she'd noticed they had stepped it up a bit. Jamie also hadn't missed that by the sixth strike, Bree had been trying to push against his hold to lift her bottom toward the blows. *God, she is absolutely fucking perfect.*

Just as he ran this hand through her slick and swollen pussy lips for the second time, he pushed his middle finger deep inside her pulsing channel and said, "Come for us, Bree." He was thankful he already had a solid hold on her because she had nearly bucked herself off his lap as her release broke loose. Her orgasm seemed to start at her core before vibrating its way to the surface in less than a second. She screamed as she came, and for the second time that day, Jamie was very grateful the suites in the ShadowDance mansion and The Club had all been soundproofed.

Jamie continued to hold her as she slowly started to surface from her orgasm. When she seemed to be approaching a point where rational thought might have been possible, he watched as Ethan reached under her and knew his friend had pinched her clit when he leaned close to her ear and simply said, "Again."

Bree was thrown right back over the edge into an abyss

of pleasure, and this time, he'd been better prepared and held even more securely anchored to him. When he finally felt her sag in exhaustion, he turned her and cradled her in his lap as Ethan helped him remove her clothing.

Brushing her tears away and kissing her sweetly, he told her how proud he was of the way she'd taken her punishment and how beautiful she'd come for them as well. And even though they hadn't planned to make love to her tonight, there wasn't a doubt in his mind that was exactly what they were going to do.

Chapter 16

ETHAN WATCHED AS Jamie cuddled Bree and whispered what he was sure were words of praise into her ear. He'd been shocked at how well she'd taken her punishment, but then again, it merely confirmed they'd been right all along. Bree was a natural submissive and the fact that she was already curious about the lifestyle was a huge bonus.

She'd come beautifully on command—*twice*. He wondered how long it had been since she had given herself a release because the two she'd had moments ago had to have been mind-bending in their intensity. His cock was so hard, he wasn't sure he'd be able to walk across the room to the bed without doing some kind of permanent damage, but he was damned well going to try. Leaning over, he nodded once to Creed before scooping up their beauty and making his way to the enormous quilt-covered bed.

"You, my love, are amazing," Ethan whispered close to her ear. "You took your punishment so beautifully, then came for both of your masters immediately upon their command. You have pleased us both very much." He felt the shudder that skittered up her spine and smiled when she looked up into his eyes. Feeling his heart clench at the lost look he saw hovering, he leaned forward and kissed the tear tracks on her flushed cheeks.

"We want to make love to you. We won't do anything you aren't ready for, but we also want to start preparing you to take us both at the same time." Searching her sweet face for any trace of hesitation, he let out the breath he hadn't even realized he was holding when she didn't offer any resistance.

He had held her long enough for to Jamie turn down the bed, so he was able to lay her gently on the sheets. Hearing the rustle of clothing behind him, he knew Creed was undressing, so he took time to smooth back her silken curls. Her hair was the color of spun gold, and he was pleased when she turned her face further into his touch.

"Do you wear the contacts for vision correction or just to alter the color of your eyes?" He knew his question had startled her because he saw more than heard her quick intake of breath.

"My vision is fine, but… well, my eye color is fairly distinctive, the contacts are required to conceal that." She had responded so slowly, he wondered at first if she was going to answer him at all. He hadn't been surprised by her reply, but he found himself saddened by it.

"Well, Love, beginning tomorrow, Master Jamie and I would like for you to leave them out. It's better for the health of your eyes, but more importantly, it's important for you to be yourself. We'll leave the issue with your name up to you, but my guess is you'll want to keep your new one rather than tackling the nearly impossible task of reversing a declaration of death." He also assumed she wanted to maintain the distance she'd established from her parents, but that was a topic for another day. Pleased at her slow nod, he stood up and moved back to undress and watched as Jamie lay down next to her.

Ethan had always appreciated how easily the two of

them worked together. As snipers, they'd been one of the best teams the military had produced in two generations, largely because they could anticipate each other's actions and reactions to within a fraction of a second. It had been obvious from the beginning, they were both good, but once they'd become partners in sniper school, they'd become practically invincible.

He and Jamie stayed partners during their entire tenure in the military, racking up a success rate that would likely endure for years to come. While Ethan knew on a cognitive level their work had contributed to the safety of a lot of people, his heart understood Jamie's concern about the cosmic debt they'd racked up. He'd wondered at times if their inability to find a woman to share was the Universe's way of evening the score. Pushing those dark thoughts to the back of his mind, he refocused his attention on the naked woman arching toward Creed's gentle touch.

Ethan had gotten lost in thought and didn't remember getting undressed. He was grateful for Bree's soft, lust-filled sighs because they'd brought him back to the moment and focused his attention on the needs her body was so blatantly displaying. Her breasts weren't huge, but their peaked baby-pink nipples were begging for attention, and he was more than happy to oblige.

Positioning himself on her other side, Ethan swiped his tongue over the beaded flesh before blowing a puff of air over first one taut nipple and then the other. Smiling when goosebumps raced along the surface of her beautiful skin, Ethan was thrilled to learn her nipples were sensitive; it would make decorating them later even more fun.

Watching Creed slide down between her thighs to use his slender fingers to open the engorged lips of her labia, Ethan felt her shudder and smiled as her need seemed to be pulsing all around them. Ethan pulled back from lavishing attention on her nipples to admire her bare mons. God how he loved being able to see even the smallest muscle twinge and every sweet drop of a sub's honey as it flowed from her depths.

"We love your waxed pussy, baby. It's a something we hope you'll consider continuing." Ethan felt her tense and wondered if he'd overstepped some unseen boundary. Bree slowly opened her eyes and met his gaze directly.

"It isn't waxed. It's... well, it's lasered, so it's permanent." Ethan knew Jamie had frozen at her words just as he had. When they both just continued watching her, she went on to explain she and a couple of her college friends had undergone the treatments as a sort of sorority bonding activity a couple of years earlier during an extended reunion trip through Europe. While he was thrilled with the results, the thought of her exposing herself to multiple clinicians was enough to make him see red. If she belonged to him, no one would see her naked without either him or Creed in the room. Barely tamping down his urge to voice his opinion, Ethan simply smiled at her and was happy with his decision when he saw her visibly relax.

JAMIE'S EYES HADN'T left hers from the moment she'd first started explaining how she'd come to be bare and smooth under his tongue, but now his cock was demanding its due and the need to explore was just too much to ignore.

"Fuck! I want to see it all, *Chère*. Lift your legs." When she started to pull her knees together, he shook his head. "No, keep them apart." Jamie knew Ethan was watching each of her reactions as he lifted her legs and saw there wasn't a hair to be found, hell, she'd even done her legs.

"Unbelievable. Well, I have to say this is a most welcome surprise, sweetness." Refocusing his attention on her face, he slid back up until they were face to face. "Your skin is so very beautiful. If you were draped in white silk, you'd look like the angel my *grand-mère* kept in her reading room." Smoothing his hands down and then back up her toned legs, he exerted just enough pressure to make sure she understood his need for the touch.

"She saw you, you know? The last time I was home, she told me you were on your way to me. Her gift of 'the second sight' has always been particularly accurate when it comes to me. I can hardly wait for you to meet her."

Jamie knew Bree was struggling to track his words. He also knew she was failing in a big way, and that was exactly as he'd intended. Never allowing his hands to stop moving, he used a technique similar to tantric massage Doms often used with newbie subs who were having difficulty focusing during their first foray into public scenes. The purpose was to ensure the sub was so lost in the sensations the Dom was providing, their minds could finally let go and allow their bodies to take over. That moment of complete surrender was always sweet, and with Bree, it was going to be even better.

A true submissive was easy for Jamie to read, and Bree's submission went bone deep. The caretaker portion of her personality and her desire to please those around her were at the very core of who she was, and those traits were almost always found in true submissives.

"*Chère*, I want you to keep your eyes open and on mine. I want to look into their depths as I fuck you. No matter what Master Ethan does, I want you to keep your eyes open, do you understand?" Even though they had already started the scene earlier, he knew she'd hear the shift in his voice from lover to Dom.

"Yes, Sir. I understand." At her words, her eyelids fluttered open, and he was enthralled with the desire he saw reflected in their depths.

Un-fucking-believable—I can't believe God's grace—she is an answered prayer.

He was grateful he'd already rolled on the condom Ethan handed him, so he didn't need to move from between her thighs. Using the tip of his throbbing cock, he teased her slick pussy lips. When she moaned and started to close her eyes he growled. Her eyes opened wide and locked on his.

"Good girl." He slid in slow and steady until he was fully seated balls-deep in her heat. Jamie didn't waste any time, setting a fast pace he knew would push her close to the edge. Just as he felt her nearing the point of no return, he rolled onto his back, taking her with him. She was startled enough by the move, Jamie knew he'd brought her back from her impending orgasm. He watched as Ethan laid the lube and a small butt plug on the bed and leaned close to speak against her ear.

"Love, lie down on Master Jamie's chest. I'm going to start stretching this beautiful ass, so you'll be able to take us both. You may feel a small pinch and a bit of a burn, but I'm going to go very slowly, so you won't be in any real pain. I want you to remember you have a safe word. If you use it, everything stops, and we discuss things." She was already lying over Jamie's chest, and he'd banded her tightly to him with one arm while he massaged slow circles over her lower back with his other hand.

Jamie had to hold back his chuckle when she gasped

and whined that the lube was cold. He leaned close to her ear and whispered, "You aren't going to be cold for long, sweetheart, I promise." He could feel Ethan's finger through the thin membrane separating them and was pleased to know he'd been able to breach her tight ring of muscles without her crying out. The plug Ethan had brought to the bed was small enough the hard part was over.

Ethan nodded to him over her shoulder, and Jamie immediately started sliding in and out of her sheath. He'd raised her up enough he was able to see her eyes were glazed with desire. Suddenly, she became much tighter and Jamie knew Ethan had started pushing the plug into place. Bree's eyes rolled back, and she groaned, giving herself over fully to the pleasure. Jamie was so overtaken by the sweet sounds she was making and the way her body was responding to his, he didn't have the heart to correct her for closing her eyes.

"*Chère*, I want you to let yourself fly. Reach for the stars, baby. Come for me." The second he spoke the words, it felt like her entire body clenched around him. She called out both of their names as she came, and when she collapsed against his chest, he could feel their hearts pounding as one.

Jamie heard Ethan speaking to her softly after he returned with a cloth from the bathroom. He was grateful for Ethan's words of praise because he still hadn't recovered his own ability to speak yet. Bree had turned him completely inside out and drained not only every ounce of energy from his now thoroughly sated body, but she'd also proven, yet again, how perfectly she completed the two of them.

When Ethan lifted her from Jamie's body, he moved to

the bathroom. Disposing of the condom, he quickly cleaned himself up before returning to the bedroom. Standing at the side of the large bed, he watched as she slept peacefully in Ethan's arms. Sending up a silent prayer of thanks for God's grace, Jamie slipped back between the sheets and curled himself against her warm back. As he drifted to sleep, he realized he honestly couldn't remember a time when he'd felt more exhausted, yet completely at peace.

Chapter 17

One week later

BREE LEANED BACK against the warm rock and watched as her new friends did the same. Thank God, Kat had been able to find a swimsuit that fit Bree or she probably would have skipped the "Girls' Night In" party and missed all the craziness that lay at the heart of these women. She'd laughed so hard, she was sure her stomach muscles were going to burn like all hell tomorrow, but it would still be worth it.

Just as Bree was thinking about closing her eyes, Rissa said, "Oh no you don't, girlfriend! You just pry those crazy gray eyes of yours right on back open. If you're gonna drink in front of me—which is just plain mean by the way—you are at least gonna spill about those two hotties you're sleeping with."

Bree heard Kat snort with laughter just before she blurted, "God bless Bess, Rissa! You made margarita come out my nose. Damn and double damn, that shit burns ya know." The giggle that accompanied her words made it clear she wasn't angry at her pregnant friend.

"Well, it serves your skinny ass right. Drinking in front of me is just… well, it's just plain rotten, I'm telling you." Rissa leaned back and looked down at her rounded belly and sighed. "I'm a whale. And I'm not even close to my due date. I'm going to be able to roll faster than I can walk before the end of the month. No one will want to go anywhere with me for fear I'll become a runaway human battering ball. Women and children will run screaming in fear. Hell, I'll end up on the news... Nancy Grace will do a show about me... you just watch and see. Oh, and someone will video it with their super-duper fucking cell phone, and it'll go viral in half a blink and when you all Google my name, that's the first thing that will pop up. Shit, see what's happened? I've gotten all off track. Pregnancy brain is real. I swear my mind wanders so often it should probably have its own tracking device." Then turning back to Bree, she smiled before whispering, "Out with it. Are you still being tag-teamed, or are you getting twofers yet?"

This time it was Jenna who laughed and said, "Damn, Rissa, you're using up punches on your 'I'm pregnant and can get away with anything' card pretty early, aren't you? Hell, even Kat had the good sense—usually—to wait until her seventh month."

"Hey! I resemble that remark!" Kat splashed her best friend and sister-in-law but was obviously having trouble working up any real steam. "And you all might want to keep in mind my sweet husbands have this place wired for sight and sound to an extent I heard the CIA is sending people out here for training. Frack! If you burp, they're going to know what you had for lunch two days ago. Shit! I'm going to be in so much trouble for all these margaritas, but I've been waiting for one of these parties forever! Between being pregnant, then breastfeeding, ugh." Then turning to Rissa, she added, "And my skinny ass, as you so indelicately referred to my lush derriere, is the result of breastfeeding *three* children... not one, not two, but *three*!

Granted most of it was done in my sleep but still."

Bree couldn't help the giggle that escaped, and just as she thought she had herself under control, the others joined in, and before long, they were all rolling around like loons howling with laughter.

MITCH GRAYSON WATCHED the monitors from the Crow's Nest and shook his head even as he chuckled to himself. Damn, but the women never ceased to make his day when they had these parties. The bosses made sure their little get-togethers were closely monitored after they'd nearly lost Kat when a sniper took a shot at her during a party in her suite. He didn't have a doubt in the world the feeds were also being monitored by Jenna's husband, Colt, both Alex and Zach Lamont as well as Creed and Jantz. They were probably all gathered in the Lamonts' office, so they'd be close in case things went from sunshine to shit as they often seemed to when their women got together.

Mitch knew Rissa didn't expect Bryant back until next weekend, and that accounted for at least a good portion of her snark because it was unusual for her to be so out of sorts. He also knew that wasn't all of it, but the blasted woman had learned to block him unless she was really distracted, so he was grateful that Bry would be home any minute.

Bryant could definitely distract her, then Mitch would be able to find out what was happening in his sweet wife's life that was making her so abrasive of late. Mitch's empathetic gifts had always been a mixed blessing. He was learning quickly how hard it was to deal with his and

Bryant's pregnant sub after she'd learned how to block him.

Shaking his head, Mitch wondered how the hell his friends were able to handle their women without being able to literally hear their thoughts. Hell, it was no wonder the divorce rate was so high in the vanilla world. At least in Ds relationships, Doms could demand honesty, and while it wasn't a guarantee the sub would be truthful, it sure put them ahead of the game.

Bree's small, pink phone was lying on the desk beside him, and when it beeped, he answered it without even checking the caller ID. After he'd said "Grayson," he heard a small gasp, then he was flooded with a feeling of cold-hearted emptiness that stole his breath.

Chapter 18

CHRISTINA GILLETTE WAS surprised when her daughter's phone didn't roll to voice mail and was completely floored that it had been answered by a man. What the hell was going on? Well, in her experience the best defense was always a good offense, so she jumped in with both feet.

"Well, Mr. Grayson, may I ask who you are exactly? Where is my daughter? I've been trying to get in touch with her for several days. I'd like to speak with her, immediately."

Mitch had been so stunned by the feeling of complete emptiness rolling off the woman who had identified herself as Bree's mother, he didn't answer her right away. He'd already known the woman was a bitch of the first order, but he hadn't been prepared for the feelings he was drowning in.

How the hell did sweet Bree grow up around this woman and become the caring and compassionate soul that she is? Holy shit, this woman is straight-up evil.

When she barked her questions a second time, he hit the record button, then the signal alert that would bring in backup. Those things done, he answered, "I'm a friend of Bree's. She isn't available to take your call right now. I can give her a message."

He knew in an instant why she'd called, the tracker they'd removed from Bree's shoulder last week was on its way to Guatemala with a member of their team. Of course, they'd already downloaded all the data before they'd sent it on, and the tiny bit of technology had been a treasure trove of information.

The plethora of information on arms sales around the world included the names of both buyers and sellers, along with dates and places of meetings. Someone was definitely *in the know*, and there was no question why she wanted it back. When Alex had decided to send Trenton Walker on a routine fact-finding mission, he'd volunteered to take the now-blank chip and tracker with him.

Their hope had been the strange destination would flush out whoever was watching Bree, and it appeared to have brought at least part of the pond scum to the surface. Mitch heard the woman sigh in frustration before she finally deemed him worthy of a response.

"Well, as I said, I've been trying to get in touch with her for days. Please have her call me immediately. Oh… and Mr. Grayson? Where exactly are you?"

Oh, very subtle, Ms. Spook, but I didn't just fall off the turnip truck this morning you know. No, indeed. Jesus, this woman is cold clear to the bone. There isn't an ounce of love anywhere in her.

"Well, Mrs. Gillette, I'd rather you spoke to Bree about our location. I'll be sure to let her know you are looking for her. Oh, and Mrs. Gillette?"

The woman's exasperation was clear in her curtly spoken "Yes?"

"You and I both know you have been trying to get in touch with Bree for a lot longer than a week. You might find honesty would be a unique, yet effective way to deal with your daughter in the future."

He heard her cursing as he disconnected the call. For long minutes, he sat documenting, not only the content of the call but also his impressions. He'd discovered as a young child waiting until he could share information often resulted in a significant dilution of the details. As he wrote about the coldness of the woman's emotions, he was suddenly aware she was the alpha in her pseudo-marriage, and Bree's father was more of a pawn than a participant in his wife's life of intrigue. Once he'd finished his report, he forwarded the encrypted file to Alex. After his backup arrived, he made his way down to speak with his bosses personally.

When he shared the phone call with the other members of the team, they agreed sending the tracker out of the country had obviously lit a fire under at least one group of bogeys. Chuckling, they surmised they'd likely have company in the very near future.

BRYANT DAVIS DROVE up the long drive leading to The ShadowDance Club, anticipating a reunion with his beautiful wife. He hadn't seen Rissa in three long weeks and was about ready to hump a tree. The bridge project he'd been working on in Japan when he'd first met the woman who now owned his heart and soul had led to an exponential growth in his business. It was time to bring in a partner *or three*.

Parking in front of The Club, he made his way quickly up the stairs and into the gardens. He'd gotten a text from Mitch just a few minutes earlier and knew Rissa was still with her friends in the pool area at the base of the waterfall. The location was a favorite of the women, and the security team was grateful the unruly group didn't bounce around the estate because they'd upped the security in this area to a point birds and insects were afraid to enter.

Just as he was ready to round the corner that would make him visible to the women, he heard his name, so he stopped and listened. He recognized Katarina Lamont's voice.

"Well, Rissa, when are you going to be getting some of that twofer action you were asking Bree about? Bryant's been gone for a while. When is that gorgeous hubby of yours supposed to be home?"

He knew his mouth had dropped open, but he kept still and waited to hear Rissa's answer.

"Well... not for... damn! I promised myself I wasn't gonna cry about this again today. I'm so scared, he's gone all the time since I got pregnant. I know I'm huge and not really desirable, right now, but I miss him so much. Even if he doesn't want to fuck me right now, I... well, I still need him to hold me, know what I mean?"

Bryant had to reach out his hand to steady himself against a tree. Never in a million years had it even crossed his mind Rissa would think he was traveling to avoid her. And while a part of him wanted to paddle her ass for even entertaining such a crazy notion, a larger part of him wanted to wrap his arms around her and soothe away each insecure thought racing through her sweet body and soul.

He'd known pregnant women could be more emotional than normal—hell, he and Grayson had read every one of the pregnancy books Katarina had so gladly handed over. Realizing both he and Mitch had totally missed something this important to their little sub was enough to make him consider retaking the beginner's class at The Club. Knowing Mitch would certainly have heard her comments and was no doubt headed down the back stairs at a dead run, Bryant reached into one of the hidden bins to grab one of the subbie blankets hidden inside, then turned and headed straight toward his sweet woman.

It was time to show her just how much he'd missed her, too and how much he did not appreciate her referring to herself as a whale.

Oh, my darling Rissa, you may be pregnant, but that isn't going to keep me from giving you a few stinging swats to your beautifully bare ass before I send you over the moon with an orgasm unlike anything you've ever experienced before.

Chapter 19

Bree had watched attentively as Rissa was happily reunited with her husband. The red-haired beauty had hastily introduced them, and Bree had swooned right along with the other women when both Bryant and Mitch had leaned down to kiss Rissa's baby bump before whisking her away. It had only taken minutes for Alex Lamont to appear and help Kat from the pool. Even though he'd been scolding her about her language and her "state of inebriation" as he'd called it, his deep love and respect for his wife was plain to see.

Mia Marshall had been quiet all evening. Bree asked her how she was feeling several times, and Mia still didn't seem aware that she was in the early stages of labor. When she'd notice Mia wince in pain, Bree decided it was time to be a bit more "direct" in her questioning.

"Mia, I know we don't know each other all that well, but I wanted to make sure you are aware you're in labor." She saw the dark-haired beauty go a bit pale, so she quickly added, "It is probably going to be hours before you need to make your way to the hospital, but I wanted you to know, I'll be available in case you need anything."

Bree wasn't surprised to see tears fill the other woman's dark eyes. No doubt she was feeling swamped by vulnerability and apprehension. Bree had always made it a point to stay very close to first-time mothers in labor because the same emotions seemed to prevail in all cultures. If Kat was right about the area being "wired for sound," Bree didn't doubt that the cavalry was already on its way.

Jenna moved over to sit next to Mia and smiled at both women before speaking. "Well, as you know, my brothers and their team have a sound system that picks up even the smallest confession, so no doubt they have already alerted Dylan and the local EMS, and if I was a betting woman, I'd expect to see Zach and his medical bag rounding the corner in… three… two… one…" Bree and Mia both leaned their heads back and roared with laughter as Zach Lamont came skidding around the corner with his black medic's bag in hand. Jenna just smiled and shrugged.

His puzzled "What?" sent them all into another round of giggles. He quickly waved both Jenna and Bree to the side and began checking Mia. It amused Bree he seemed to have forgotten she was a physician. When Mia started to protest, Bree got to witness firsthand that Zach Lamont could easily be every bit the intimidating Dom she knew his brother to be.

No sooner had Colt, Ethan, and Jamie arrived than Dylan Marshall came running around the corner hedge shouting, "Where in the hell is my wife?" When he saw her reclining along the rock edge of the pool, he scooped her up into his arms and after he'd settled her on his lap, he started stroking her back in gentle circles. Bree stood back, watching as the tall man was reduced to near tears as he brushed kisses on Mia's face. It would be obvious to even the most casual observer, the love between the two former DEA agents ran soul-deep.

After the ambulance pulled away with Mia and Dylan

inside, Colt leaned down and whispered in Jenna's ear, causing her to flush a deep crimson. Bree had seen similar interactions among couples from several continents, and it was almost always for the same reason. As she, Jamie, and Ethan were making their way back to the suite, she leaned toward the men and whispered, "Wanna make a bet with me?" She hiccupped, then grinned at their frowns.

Hmm, probably maybe shoulda not gulped down that last margarita during all the pandemonium.

"Yeah, yeah... so I had a couple of margaritas... cope. Now, how about that bet? Or are you afraid of losing some money to a woman?" She giggled when they turned as if following directions of some invisible conductor and glared at her.

"So, *ma Chère*, what is it you are wanting to bet on?" Bree started to lean back against the door, intending to look cool and casual. But she had misjudged the distance and would have tumbled straight back onto her ass if Jamie hadn't reached forward and grabbed her arms. "Whoa there, sweetness, perhaps you need to sit down while we discuss this bet and just exactly what you are willing to wager."

As he led her to the small sitting area, she saw him look at Ethan and wink. *Ha... I so have this one. And the rat bastards think I'm too fried, oops, I mean toasted to know what I'm doing.* When she found herself sitting on Jamie's lap she looked up.

"I want to bet that Jenna is pregnant and they haven't told anyone yet." Realizing what she'd done, she slapped herself on the forehead. "Shit! I'm not supposed to tell you that until you say you'll bet me, am I? Damn those margaritas were strong. Kat is a wicked bartender, I tell you!"

She started giggling again and saw the men exchange a

look she couldn't interpret. Deciding that caution wasn't all it was cracked up to be, and that she might just as well jump in with both feet, she blurted out, "I was gonna bet you a twofer. That's what the girls call it when... well, you know." Ethan reached forward and caught her chin with his fingers, bringing her attention to him.

"No, Love, I'm not sure we do know, so why don't you explain exactly what that is. Enlighten us."

She was pretty sure they were messing with her, but she decided to humor them just in case because she was all about education.

"Well, just so you know, I think you are *mucking* with me, but I've decided to play along. Anyway, that's what they call it when one man puts his cock in a woman's pussy and the other one..." When she hiccupped again, she had to focus her eyes again. *What the heck is that about? Since when do the hiccups make your eyesight fuzzy?* "Anyway, the other guy puts his cock in her ass. You know, like you've been yic-yakking about for a week. They have all done that... well, I guess I don't know about Mia 'cuz she was pretty quiet all day, but the others were just founts of information. Hey! I said fount. Oh, thank God, my vocabulary is back. Holy hell, those girls are fun, but they can fairly well butcher the English language, I tell ya! Oh shit, there it went again."

JAMIE WAS BITING the inside of his mouth so hard to keep from laughing, he was sure it was going to start bleeding any second and one look at Ethan told him that his friend wasn't faring much better. God, she was completely wasted and absolutely adorable.

Ethan shook his head and coughed over his laughter before leaning close to whisper, "Well, Love, do you think you are ready for that experience? I know we have been using various plugs on you, but it may be a little painful if you aren't properly stretched. Then again, I'm thinking you have ingested enough liquid painkiller, it might work out perfectly after all. What do you think, Master Jamie?"

Jamie had been trying his damnedest to not laugh out loud at the hopeful expression on Bree's face. Pretending to give the question great consideration, he finally answered.

"I don't know. As Doms, we really shouldn't give her a 'twofer' when she's drunk. She really needs to be able to give informed consent. You know how Alex and Zach are about The Club's rule against playing after more than their two-drink maximum." Then turning back to Bree, he said, "How many margaritas did you say you had? And before you answer, let me remind you that your little *'rita party* was all recorded, live and in color. Also, you might like to know, we have been watching the feeds from the beginning because we were worried about you. We didn't know how you would react to the kick-ass drinks we know Kat is famous for concocting, so we wanted to keep a close eye on you."

Bree reached her hand up and placed her palm on the side of his face and slowly stroked her fingers along his cheek. "That's so sweet I think I might cry. I don't really remember how many drinks I had but not too many not to know how much I want you. I've wanted you... both of you since the first minute I saw you. You, my Cajun Angel, you know my heart recognized you the day you carried me out of hell." Then turning to Ethan, she added, "And you, my tough but loving Master Ethan, our hearts recognized each other right away, too. You know it and I know it."

Jamie could tell she was beginning to worry because they both just sat in shocked silence, staring at her for long seconds before they regained the ability to speak. He felt his own face break out in what he was sure was a doofy grin and noticed Ethan had a similar expression. He hoped their smiles told her everything she needed to know.

Oh yeah, Chère… You are definitely getting one of those twofers tonight!

Chapter 20

As soon as they had entered the suite's bathroom, Bree felt a shift in the energy or maybe that was actually the earth tilting on its axis. Suddenly everything seemed to be leaning, no, make that spinning a bit to the left. Her eyes widened when both men turned to stand in front of her with their muscular arms crossed over their powerful chests. As she let her eyes trail down their amazing bodies, she noted they both spread their legs shoulder-width apart, and the effect their posture had was surprising in its intensity.

Bree felt her pussy flood with moisture in anticipation of their possession, and a shiver raced up her spine. She knew they wouldn't have missed her gulping swallow, but she couldn't help that now. She hoped that her mental "Holy shit!" hadn't actually been said aloud, but judging by the tiny twitch she'd seen in Jamie's jaw, she was pretty sure she'd actually spoken the words. Damn.

Note to self...remember how potent Kat's margaritas are.

Both men had worked with her during the past week on various elements of the D/s lifestyle, and she'd quickly discovered there wasn't a question she could ask that would embarrass either of them, and each day she learned something else about herself. Her time at ShadowDance had been an amazing journey of self-discovery, and she had been pleasantly surprised to discover how healing each of those small revelations was.

"Strip." Ethan's quiet command surprised her because she had been concentrating so hard on not weaving. When she didn't move quickly enough, he simply raised his eyebrows, and she quickly scrambled to peel off the formfitting swimsuit she'd been wearing.

When she returned to her original position, she saw that they were both naked as well. *Wow, how long did it take me to get that damned suit off, anyway?* Bree watched as Jamie started the shower, then they both turned to her. Ethan reached out his hand, and she placed her small one in his much larger one.

"Let's get that spring water off your beautiful skin, shall we? The shower will also help sober you up a bit. Did you eat anything this afternoon? We can have a tray sent up."

As she entered the enormous shower, she turned a bit too quickly and fell against Ethan's chest. Burrowing her face against him, she sighed.

"I did eat a bit, but I'm only hungry for the two of you right now. Maybe we can eat later?" She would have sworn she heard them both growl before they set about washing her hair, just as they'd done each time they'd showered together. The feel of their hands massaging her scalp, then soaping her body was sweet torture.

JAMIE WASN'T SURE he was going to get out of the shower without fucking her up against the floor-to-ceiling windows that took up one entire wall of the enclosure. He loved the way the windows could be frosted for privacy or left crystal clear if the Dom decided his sub was in need of a bit of "display play." They hadn't taken time to frost the wall, so anyone in the garden would be getting a show right about now. The idea of pressing Bree against the glass and sliding into her sweet depths while the whole world watched them was almost more temptation than Jamie could pass up.

He and Ethan worked together to get their sweet sub washed, dried, and smothered in her sweet-smelling lotion as quickly as possible. Taking note of the small incision on her shoulder, Jamie was pleased to see the minor wound was almost completely healed. Watching as Ethan combed through her tangled hair, Jamie was almost overcome by a feeling of satisfaction he'd never known before Bree had come into their lives. As his *grand-mère* would say, *"The light that shines from inside her warms all those it touches."*

Damn, he could hardly wait to introduce his two favorite women to each other. He and Ethan had talked about taking some time off. They both wanted to take Bree to meet their families as soon as it was safe for her to travel, and he was getting antsy for that time to arrive.

Ethan's voice brought Jamie's thoughts back to the moment, and he smiled when he heard his friend tell Bree exactly how he wanted to find her when they returned to the bedroom. Laughing at her gasp when Ethan sent her on her way with a swat to her rosy ass, Jamie still marveled at the primitive conditions Bree had lived in for so much of her life. She'd grown surrounded by abject poverty and clearly didn't put much stock in material things.

He and Ethan had both been shocked when they learned that everything she owned was in her small car. Alex and Zach had brought in three small suitcases the day she'd arrived. And according to the Lamonts, her small car had also held a small box of books and another smaller box containing a few personal mementos that looked like things made by children, and that was the extent of her belongings. Christ, it had taken him three trips with his SUV to move his younger sister to college, and she'd barely made a dent in her room at home.

When they stepped into the bedroom, Jamie nearly swallowed his tongue at the sight. Bree was bent over at the waist with her feet spread far apart with her hands grasping the wooden end board on the large bed. Her back was arched perfectly, and when she turned to look at them, her expression was one of anticipation and excitement. Gone was the wary and skittish woman they'd met so recently. He and Ethan were both thrilled with the way Bree seemed to blossom under their dominance. The change in her self-confidence level was very gratifying.

Looking over at Ethan, Jamie knew his friend was falling for Bree just as he was. Jamie was grateful Alex was working to get Bree's medical license in her new name, but as far as he was concerned, Alex's inevitable success would be a mixed blessing. On the positive side was the joy Bree found in caring for those in need, but he also worried she would want to move to a larger city in order to establish a practice. Deciding to set those thoughts aside, Jamie stepped closer to Bree and ran his hand down the satiny smooth skin covering her spine and smiled as she moaned softly and arched into his touch. He murmured, "Beautiful," and Ethan heartily agreed.

WHEN ETHAN STEPPED into the bedroom and took in the

beautiful woman so perfectly displayed before him, he felt all the blood drain out of his brain and race south. He was so blown away by the stunning vision, it hadn't been until Jamie had stepped forward that Ethan had been able to surface from the lustful trance he'd fallen into.

Even though he'd agreed with Jamie's assessment that Bree was beautiful, the word was vastly inadequate to describe how heart-stopping she was. She was, quite simply, radiant. There was just something about the woman that spoke to him on such a primal level, Ethan wasn't even sure he could describe it to anyone.

He'd been sitting on the back deck late last night when Zach Lamont had joined him. After discussing trivial bullshit for several minutes, Zach had looked directly into his eyes.

"It blows you away doesn't it?" At first, Ethan had been so surprised by the question he hadn't responded. Zach had assumed he hadn't understood and added, "When *the one* walks into your life—it knocks the blocks out from under you, doesn't it? I just wanted you to know, Alex and I understand, and we'll help in any way we can. Our mom has told us a lot about Bree's past, and we know you and Creed are helping her overcome her fears. Don't be afraid to seek advice if you need it. If neither Alex nor I can help, we'll find someone who can. She's special. Mom and Kat both love her, and that alone speaks volumes, but the night she came up to the nursery to check on our children was the night it all gelled for Alex and me as well.

"Did you know she came back up twice during the night? How she got out of that suite without waking either of you is nothing short of a miracle. Personally, I think we should hire her for the teams."

Ethan was shocked to learn she'd been able to leave the

room without waking them. Christ, they were among the world's most sought-after operatives, and they'd let a civilian leave their watch not once but twice in *one* night?

As if sensing the direction his thoughts had turned, Zach leaned forward and clasped his shoulder. "Don't go there, brother. She walked down the hall and back because she was concerned for our children—don't you dare punish her for *loving*. When Alex and I questioned her, she assured us you both needed your rest more than you needed to walk those few feet with her. She agreed to beep the intercom once before coming again, and she did, so we were waiting outside her door the second time."

Ethan knew he'd sighed in relief, but it still stuck in his craw he'd been bested by the little beauty he was falling in love with. Zach had leaned back and as if reading his mind, said, "It'll be okay, you know. She's falling for you two as well. Just see how it plays out, but I have a great feeling about this one."

After Zach had gone back inside, Ethan had smiled into the darkness and thought back to the only time he'd ever met Jamie's *grand-mère*. The damned woman wasn't even five feet tall and yet she had a presence that filled any room she entered. She'd walked out onto the porch one evening and placed her hand on Ethan's arm and said, *"When the Universe sends your angel, save her and then let her save you,"* then she just walked away. He'd been left with the impression the Universe had sent him a messenger that night, and he'd felt the same tonight as he'd watched Zach walk away.

Now, standing beside Bree as she maintained her position while Jamie stroked the length of her spine, he was humbled by the gift of her submission. He'd never wanted to please and protect a woman as much as he wanted to with Bree Hart. She was, without question, the missing piece of the puzzle that had become his life. For the first time he could remember, he was worried a woman would be repulsed by his family's wealth, rather than attracted to it. And despite her obvious lack of community standing and "name," he was sure his family was going to love her because there was such an innate goodness in her, it called to everyone who came in contact with her.

Shaking off his musings, Ethan refocused his attention on the woman in front of him. She was already trembling with need, but he and Creed were planning to push her a lot further before they launched her into sub-space.

Chapter 21

BREE FELT HER pussy flexing in response to Jamie's feather-light touch. Even though he was only faintly dragging his fingers up and back down her spine, her body had become so attuned to both men, their mere presence was usually enough to make her panties wet. Of course, she wasn't wearing panties right now thanks to The Panty Bandits aka Alex and Zach Lamont. Well hell, she'd been sure the shower she'd taken would counteract all the alcohol she'd consumed, but it seemed her askew sense of humor was still dancing down the streets of Margaritaville.

She caught herself before she giggled at her own mental joke, or at least she thought she'd merely thought it until Ethan leaned down and spoke so near her ear, she felt his warm breath caress her already sensitized skin.

"Of course, you aren't wearing panties, Love, you were told to be naked and in exactly this position. And I'm sure Alex and Zach will enjoy their new titles. You look lovely, by the way. I'm not sure what you meant about Margaritaville, but we'll give you a pass on that one this once because we're both Jimmy Buffett fans."

Bree thought there had been an underlying tone of amusement in his voice, but she wasn't sure. At least he didn't appear angry, and that had to be a plus. She groaned when she felt Jamie's hand leave her back, but Ethan was still close.

"He's not leaving, sweet sub, he is just making sure we have everything we'll need to make this enjoyable for all of us."

Bree felt her knees turn to rubber when Ethan slowly moved his fingers through the soft petals of her labia and drew lazy circles around her slick opening. When he pulled the upper shell of her ear between his teeth and gently bit down, she felt a flood of moisture and knew it must have washed over his fingers before it began slowly trickling down her inner thigh.

"Oh my, you are so wet for your Masters, and I can't begin to tell you how much that pleases us both. Now, Master Jamie is in position, so I want you to crawl up on the bed and follow his directions. Can you do that for me, my sweet Bree?"

"Y–yes, M–Master Ethan." Before she had actually managed to move, Ethan had taken his fingers and using her own juices as lubricant he pushed a finger just inside her rear entrance.

"This is mine tonight, Bree. I'm going to fuck your sweet ass while Master Jamie fucks your hot little pussy. We're going to show you exactly what it means to be our woman. Are you ready for our possession, Love? Are you ready for the ultimate submission? Know this, my love, after tonight, there'll be no turning back. After tonight, you will belong to Master Jamie and I, both. It might not be 'official' or legal—yet, but it will be just as real. Is that what you want, baby?"

Bree's vision blurred with unshed tears of joy as she looked back and nodded.

"Yes, Master Ethan, that is exactly what I want. I want you both to be my Masters." Ethan pulled her against his chest, and she heard the emotion in his voice when he told her to get up on the bed and follow Master Jamie's instructions. As she crawled up onto the massive bed, she looked at Jamie and was relieved to see him smiling even though his eyes were filled with unguarded desire.

Jamie reached for her and pulled her easily onto his broad chest, his heated skin centering her as he framed her face with his large hands and brought her lips to his. Bree was immediately lost in his kiss. She felt as if he was reaching inside her and quietly stroking her soul. His kiss was pure seduction, a gentle spiral moving her steadily toward a release she wasn't sure her heart was going to survive. When he finally released her lips, he gradually raised her torso, so she was positioned on her knees with her sex directly over his cock. His tenderly spoken words sent a rush of her honeyed syrup directly to her outer pussy lips.

"Take me inside your sweet pussy, *Chère*. I want to feel your tight velvet walls wrap themselves around my cock—hugging me so tight it tests my control in ways I never believed possible. That's right, slowly now, oh yeah. You are *ma joie, mon amour*."

Even in her fog of bliss, Bree warmed to Jamie's words; being called "my joy, my love" filled her heart. She felt herself trying to speed up the pace, but his hands gripped her hips and forced her to savor each torturously slow withdrawal and reentry until she wasn't sure she could take it another moment. When Jamie finally pulled her tight against his chest and started kissing her hair, she was so aroused, she could feel her blood surging through her system and wondered if her heart was going to beat itself right out of her chest. She tried to sit up, but his arms tightened around her like steel bands.

"No, *Chère*, stay here while your other Master prepares you." She listened to his whispered instructions, letting herself float along the meandering current of Jamie's words. "Relax and let the sensations blow over you like a cool breeze on a hot summer day. That's it, go with me—let's relax in the *pirogue* as we drift through the slow-moving waters of the bayou. Let the sunshine wash over your beautiful naked skin. Feel the beads of sweat as they trickle between your bare breasts. When a soft breeze blows over us, I'll watch in wonder as your skin flushes, and the chill bumps race over your stomach before disappearing into your bare nether regions. Your breasts will swell as your nipples tighten in response to the breeze and the warm caress of his gaze."

Bree felt herself being drawn into his fantasy, his voice hypnotizing her into a state of relaxation so deep, when Ethan's lubed fingers began pushing gently but firmly into her ass, she found herself pushing out, struggling to accommodate the breach. Bree was held captive by the heat of his touch even when he began scissoring his fingers back and forth, attempting to stretch and lubricate the tight tissues. Using the gentle push and pull as a part of the fantasy, Jamie spoke close to her ear.

"Feel the soft rocking of our small canoe, *Chère*? Let the motion lull you, let it seduce you. Flow with it as if it was coming from the depths of your soul. When you surrender to the sensations, we will be able to make you soar with the wind. Are you ready to fly, *ma jolie*?"

Bree was completely immersed in the fantasy Jamie had painted so clearly in her mind, she was barely able to whisper, "Yes" before she felt Ethan's cock pressing against the outer ring of her rear hole. There was a rush of heat as the tissues were stretched by the large head of his cock, but the searing quickly morphed into need, and she found herself pressing back into him. Ethan grabbed her hips, stilling her movement, and she could hear the strain in his voice.

"No, Love, let me take you. Do not push too quickly, or you could tear the tender tissues." When she stilled, his hands tenderly caressed the globes of her ass. "That's my sweet sub, relax and remember you belong to us. Your body is ours to care for and use as we see fit, and we want this to be perfect for you, so let go and just enjoy the ride, Love."

Groaning in pleasure, Bree let herself ease into Jamie's embrace as Ethan pushed steadily in until he was fully seated in her ass. Just as her muscles were starting to tighten in response to the endorphins flooding her system, the two of them started a slow rhythmic push and plunge that kept her filled at all times. As Jamie withdraw from her pussy, Ethan would push back into her ass, ensuring one of them was buried in her at all times.

Their pace was too slow, and she started to move in a desperate attempt to get them to speed up as she felt the need for them ramping up inside her body. When Jamie pinched her nipples firmly between two fingers and growled, "Stop now, Bree, let us take you," she stilled in their arms.

"Remember, you are ours. We will fuck you as we see fit. Know that we will always provide you with what you need, even when it isn't what you want or when you don't get it as quickly as you want it."

ETHAN HAD BEEN getting perilously close to coming, and he was almost grateful to Bree for misbehaving because it provided him a much needed, albeit too brief break in the mood. Those few seconds had given him time to recover a bit. Again, they set a slow pace that was sure to have Bree squirming in no time. Nodding his head at Creed, they began slowly picking up the pace, and judging by Bree's soft moans, she was rapidly approaching the point of no return.

When he felt the first flutters of the muscles lining her anus, he leaned close to her ear and whispered, "Come now, my love." Bree screamed, her body reacting before he'd even finished speaking. Orgasm swept through her like a tidal wave, making her muscles clamp down on both his and Jamie's cocks like a vise. Ethan heard Jamie's shout and felt him stiffen on the other side of the thin membrane separating them a split second before he was washed over the edge himself. For the first time in years, Ethan saw pinpoints of light dancing behind his eyelids when he let go and tumbled over the edge into absolute bliss.

When he finally was able to catch his breath, Ethan reluctantly pulled his cock from her warm body and sagged when the loss of connection hit him like an arctic blast. When he thought his legs would hold him upright, he moved to the bathroom to clean up. Returning with a warm washcloth, he began gently cleaning Bree where she still lay sprawled over Jamie's chest like a second skin. Bree waved her hand in a lame attempt to protest, which he ignored.

"Shhh, Love. It is my privilege and my right to care for you. Please do not deny me the pleasure. You belong to us and will discover both of your Masters will take great pride in caring for their most valuable possession."

Ethan heard Jamie whispering soft words of praise, and just as he was ready to climb into the bed, his phone rang. The distinctive tone was only assigned to Alex's and Zach's cell phones, so he leaned over and answered it before it had a chance to ring a second time. Alex's tone was clipped and all business.

"Sit-Rep, my office in twenty. All three of you. We've got company." At Ethan's acknowledgment, Alex just simply disconnected.

Chapter 22

Bree was surprised when she, Ethan, and Jamie walked into Alex and Zach's office and found it already filled with people. She knew most of the people waiting for the meeting to begin but noted there were several new faces in the mix. Unconsciously, she moved closer to Jamie—in the deepest recesses of her soul, Bree knew she was always going to recognize him as her protector. When he turned to her, she was relieved to see him smile as he wrapped her in his warm embrace.

"Don't worry, *Chère*, they are all friends. See the two men standing over near the fireplace talking to the Lamonts? The tallest is Jace Garrett, a former SEAL, and even though we weren't assigned to the same team, we worked together quite often. The other man you may have heard of—that's Ian McGregor." When he saw her eyes go wide, he chuckled and added, "Yeah, I figured I wouldn't have to explain who he was, but just so you know, he is also a friend of Alex and Zach's. Did you know he recently started a very exclusive BDSM club on his private island off the coast of Virginia—*Club Isola*? You're a smart woman, given the location, can you guess what line of work most of his members are in?"

Smiling, Bree whispered, "I'm betting he knows a lot of people in Washington, DC. It sounds like his club is close enough, it's accessible, yet far enough no one will notice when a well-known senator or representative makes his way in the front door."

"Good guess, *Chère*. But just so you know, Ian's club isn't exactly easily accessed. You'd need a boat, small plane, or chopper, and once you made it onto the island, you'd need an escort to find it the first time or two. The man is a fucking genius when it comes to design, the entrance to the place so well concealed, it is almost impossible for anyone to find it on their own. When he wanted to test its vulnerabilities a few months ago, he had Alex send a team of us to see if we could make it inside without his security people knowing we were there.

"Jace is his head of security and he's put together one hell of a team. Ian and Jace were the only ones who knew we were coming, and they weren't sure when we would arrive. I have to tell you, it was the most fun I'd had *working* in a long time."

Just as Bree opened her mouth to ask if they'd made it inside, Alex called for everyone's attention. Looking up, Bree noticed that several more people had entered while Jamie had been entertaining her. Ethan was now standing beside a table covered with maps talking to a young man dressed in a deputy's uniform.

Seeing the officer made her wonder how Mia was doing since it had been several hours since she'd gone to the hospital. While it was unlikely, it was possible she'd already given birth. She didn't hear Mitch Grayson walk up behind her, so she jumped letting out a startled cry of surprise when he leaned down to speak over her shoulder.

"Dylan called about five minutes ago and said they were headed into surgery to do a Cesarean section. It seems their little man wants to parachute outta there, feet first." Bree giggled at his joke and appreciated him letting her know what was happening.

Shaking her head, Bree wondered if she would ever get used to him being able to hear her thoughts. *Damn, that must drive poor Rissa bananas.* The words had no sooner gone through her mind than Mitch leaned down again and chuckled.

"Indeed, it does, beautiful, indeed it does."

Bree had been surprised at the efficiency the men displayed during the meeting. She'd quickly learned that a "sit-rep" was a situation report, and it seemed obvious to her they had maintained their military style of communication. Geez, she'd nearly gotten dizzy trying to keep up with the acronyms. She had always thought the medical community held the title for most ridiculously unclear abbreviations, but she'd be revising that opinion now. At one point, Alex had asked her a question, and she'd just stood, looking at him with what she knew was a completely befuddled expression. When she saw the corners of his mouth twitch, she'd said, "You know, that sounded like English, but I'll be switched if I have any idea what it meant."

She might be new to the lifestyle, but even she knew her response to the intimidating Dom standing in front of her would easily make David Letterman's "Top Ten Disrespectful Sub Reponses," so she was greatly relieved when everyone in the room roared with laughter. When they all regained their composure, Alex grabbed her and gave her a big hug.

"Welcome to ShadowDance, Bree. Damn, you are going to fit right in with Katarina and Jenna—God help us. Now, what I asked, apparently in 'military speak,' was whether you know a man named Hiram Basille? A man using that name has been asking questions around town, and a woman matching your mother's description was inquiring at the diner how she could check into our local not-yet-completed bed-and-breakfast." Smiling at his brother, he added, "Damn, it's going to be handy having Layla running that place. Hell, Tori says nothing will get by her feisty friend."

Bree explained Hiram had worked with her parents for years. She'd known him as a manager or logistics person who took care of supplies for the mission camps, but she reluctantly agreed his real role was likely much more sinister. Feeling as if the world was starting to close in on her, Bree was just moving back toward Jamie when off in the distance she heard Mitch shout, "Creed! Grab her."

Darkness was closing in around the periphery of her vision like one of those early special effects used by directors in the 1940s, and just like those old movies, it didn't matter how sappy it looked, it still happened—the darkness finally claimed her.

ETHAN HAD BEEN the one to catch her because he'd already started moving when he saw her whole-body tense at Alex's mention of her mother. He knew both the mother and father had been seen in town and found it interesting Alex had only mentioned her mother. Knowing Alex Lamont as well as Ethan did, he was certain that hadn't been done without a good reason. He also didn't miss the look that passed between Mitch, Alex, and Zach as he was carrying Bree from the room. When Creed started to follow, Ethan leaned over and asked him to please stay and find out what he could. Evidently, Jamie had noted some of the same inconsistencies because he merely nodded once and returned to the meeting.

It had taken him the better part of an hour to get Bree settled and to sleep. Christ, the woman was tenacious. You would have thought he'd asked her to sleep for a week judging by the stricken look on her face when he'd insisted she lie down for a rest. He'd finally threatened to paddle her sweet ass, telling her if she was going to act like a five-year-old, then she deserved to be treated as such. When she had finally and very reluctantly agreed to obey his direct order, he reminded her she would suffer the consequences later for her hesitance. He secretly smiled when he realized just how challenging it was to top an intelligent and independent woman. He and Jamie were about to join a very elite group among their friends since most of them now had subs who presented them with these very same challenges on a regular basis.

Katarina Lamont had eluded Alex and Zach's intense searching for years before finally returning home after she was nearly beaten to death by a criminal sadist in Las Vegas. Jenna Lamont-Matthews, Alex and Zach's younger sister, had led one division of Lamont Oil before their former team leader and the current head of security for the Lamonts had finally "reined her in" as Colt often called it. The two had been tormenting each other with barbs for years. Everyone had known they were perfect for each other, and their words were merely some kind of strange *dance of deception*, but it had taken them years to realize they were soul mates.

It was Rissa Grayson-Davis who had given, not only her husbands and Doms but the entire team the most heart-stopping moments. Mitch Grayson had spent a year trying to get Rissa Murphy to even speak to him. The redhaired trouble magnet had been kidnapped by slave traders and later shot and suffered a concussion that had nearly taken her life before finally settling in with Mitch Grayson and Bryant Davis.

Smiling to himself, Ethan realized the only one of his friends to find a sub who had fallen nearly perfectly into the lifestyle was Trace Bartell. The widowed rancher had more than paid his dues when he'd lost his wife to a drunk driver several years earlier. Tori Paulson had come to Trace complete with a crazed stalker-serial killer working as a police officer in Houston, but her move into a full-time Ds relationship had been remarkably smooth.

Tori had been an up-and-coming lawyer when her career had been derailed by the lunatic who had followed her to Climax, broken into their home, and tried to kidnap her. The whole team had heard her maneuver the crazed killer into confessing when Jamie had come to her rescue and cued his mic to broadcast and record the entire conversation. How the sweet sub had managed to stay calm was still a wonder. When the man had made a move for her, she'd shot him twice with accuracy and precision that had earned her the respect of every man on the team.

As he walked back into the sit-rep, he couldn't help but shake his head. *Seems karma was going to exact its pound of flesh on the former SEALS by blessing them with difficult women.* The irony of the situation wasn't lost on him; the only one of his friends who hadn't been challenged to bring a woman into their "lovely land of kink" was the one known by every member of The ShadowDance Club as "The Gentle Giant."

When he walked up to the table, he noticed Alex and Zach were smiling at him like cats who had just swallowed the canary. His "What?" had been met with boisterous laughter.

Alex hadn't even bothered to answer, he'd simply returned his attention to the task at hand, but his smirk spoke volumes. Zach leaned closer to Ethan and said, "We are just enjoying seeing you join the team, brother." At Ethan's puzzled glare, Zach added, "the Doms with Unruly Subs Team." His friend chuckled at his own joke before adding, "Seriously, man, Bree seems solid, and she's had a hell of a rough ride. I'm glad you guys are there for her, but I'll tell you, if you hurt her, we'll set Mom loose on the two of you, and you know hell hath no fury like Catherine Lamont."

"Christ, Zach, have a heart." Zach smiled as Ethan shook his head. "We don't have any intentions of hurting her. She's perfect. She's intelligent, compassionate, and a true submissive. We'll take the bits of challenge that are a part of the package. Any progress on her medical license?"

Zach grinned from ear to ear and said, "Oh, hell yeah. Daniel and Catherine Lamont strike again. They've made calls all the way to the top, literally. They have the President making calls as well."

Ethan was so grateful, he felt a flood of emotion that truly surprised him. He'd spent so many years training in the military to keep his emotions in check, he had wondered at times if he would ever recover the ability to actually *feel* anything. Swallowing around the lump he suddenly felt in his throat he finally managed to eke out, "Thank you. We'll all be in debt to your parents, I assure you. Now, if we can just convince the lovely doctor to stay once the threats against her are neutralized."

Alex spoke up then, "I assume you and Creed noticed I didn't mention to Bree that her father is also in town?" At their nods, he continued, "We have very credible information that leads us to believe he isn't a threat to his daughter. Nor is he a willing participant in any of his wife's 'outside the box' dealings with the arms dealers."

Mitch Grayson took over from there, "Bree has questioned his involvement, she worries her mother is going to hurt him as well. Actually, 'collateral damage' is the way she sees it. Bree suspects her parents really did start out as missionaries and her mother was, in fact, the one to get them involved with a couple of European agencies. While that is close to correct, it isn't entirely accurate. Her father knew going in they'd be gathering intel, but he'd always been told it was for the UN. He'd only agreed because he'd been convinced the information was being used to block arms shipments, not facilitate them."

There wasn't a doubt in Ethan's mind there was more Mitch wasn't saying, so he decided to wait his friend out. Mitch finally looked up from the sheaf of papers in his hand, moving his gaze between Creed and Ethan.

"Fuck. Yeah, there's more. We believe Christina Gillette is being squeezed big-time. She's made some serious errors lately, letting Bree and the chip slip through her fingers just one of several. We also think she is setting up her husband to take the fall. John Gillette isn't a player in this—actually, his biggest crime is not standing up to his wife. He's turned a blind eye to her activities for years, but it seems the incident a year ago with their daughter was an eye opener for him."

Colt Matthews had been standing by, silently listening to everything being presented without adding anything since Ethan had reentered the room, so he was surprised when the man finally stepped forward.

"We want to get to John Gillette. We'll make contact

and offer him a deal. We've been authorized to offer him some pretty substantial considerations if he'll testify against his wife and Basille." Looking from Ethan to Creed, the man added, "Having Bree in on this—at least the negotiations with her dad would be a big help. What do you two think?"

"I think you are asking the wrong people, Mr. Matthews. Why don't you ask me directly, instead of placing Ethan and Jamie in the unenviable position of making a decision they can't possibly make?"

Every man in the room turned to see Bree standing in the doorway, looking every bit the formidable professional she was. And while there was a part of him that wanted to paddle her for her insolence, for the first time since he'd become a Dom, he was damned proud of a sassy sub under his control.

Chapter 23

Bree stood in the doorway listening to the men talking about her as if she were a mental patient who wasn't capable of making an informed decision on her own. Like she needed Ethan or Jamie to decide what she should do about her own father? Were they all really that arrogant? Of course, they were, they were a bunch of sexual Dominants who were also retired Navy SEALS. Hell, by anybody's definition, they ought to be the poster boys for egotism.

She struggled to maintain at least the illusion of decorum and had thought she was doing a fine job until Mitch Grayson broke out in a wide grin. *Damned empaths anyway! I swear to all that is holy, his wife has to be the most patient woman on the planet. It must be beyond a pain in the ass to have him poking around in her head all the time.*

Damn it, Bree, focus! These guys can smell fear, don't let them scare you. You've dealt with the dark side, and these guys don't play for that team.

She stood her ground waiting for them to answer her, and the longer she waited, the more annoyed she became. When Ethan's posture shifted to Dom, she saw Mitch reach over and still him with a touch on his arm. Mitch didn't take his eyes from hers and spoke softly, trying to hide his amusement, and that wasn't sitting well with her either.

"Bree, you are right, it is important that we get your input, but we thought you were resting, so we asked your men their opinion. You are also right that my gift makes Rissa crazy sometimes, but it also helps me get to the heart of matters in a hurry. So, I want you to hear well what I'm telling you; none of us ever wants you to fear us except in all the good kinky ways. You've already had more than your share of dealing with the dark side of humanity, and we would all like to help you put those pieces of your life behind you. What do you say, sweetie? You in or out?"

Ethan hadn't been that crazy about his friend referring to his woman as "sweetie," but considering her entire body seemed to sag in relief and a slow smile swept over her face—now that he hadn't expected—perhaps he'd cut Grayson some slack, this time.

Jamie stepped in front of Bree and took her hand. "*Chère*. Neither Ethan nor I will ever deny you the opportunity to have input in important decisions. I promise you the only time your opinion won't weigh in as equal is when we're playing or when your safety is in question. Do you understand?"

"Yes, I understand, but I want to be kept informed about my parents. For what it's worth, I would also like to help. I agree with your assessment of my dad's involvement. I know you haven't seen the real strength that is at the heart of me, you've only seen the 'victim' and the 'recovering victim,' you haven't seen the pushy woman I can be. And while I love having you ready to catch me if I fall and having you go all Alpha-Male trying to protect me is wonderful... sometimes, well, most of the time, please don't coddle me so much, the strong woman I once was doesn't ever resurface."

As Ethan and Jamie closed in on her, their smiles eased her anxiety about having overstepped her bounds. But it was Zach Lamont's laughing words that touched her heart.

"Damn but I love spirited women. Hope those two knuckleheads know what a great gift they've been given."

AS THE MEETING was breaking up, Bree looked up to see Kat and Jenna standing at the door of the office. They were waiting patiently, but she wasn't sure exactly who or what they were waiting for. Before she could ask Ethan, she saw Alex's almost imperceptible nod.

Both women immediately rushed to her side and must have read her look of confusion because Kat leaned forward and said, "Come on, girlfriend, time for a break." Then leaning closer she whispered, "We'll explain, I promise." Before Bree realized what was happening, she was sitting at the bar in the kitchen between the two women, watching as Selita whipped up a *snack* for the three of them.

Kat leaned over, giving her a shoulder bump. "That was a 'need to know' only meeting, and as my loving husbands often remind me, I don't have the security clearance to 'need to know.' Neither does my bestie over there, so we've learned to just wait at the door for him to give us the go-ahead to enter. Keeps us from having to stand for several days if you get my drift."

Both Kat and Jenna laughed, and it took Bree a few seconds to catch on they were talking about the spankings they'd obviously gotten before they'd learned to wait for permission to enter the Doms' domain.

"Yeah, I love an erotic spanking as much as anyone, but damn, those punishment spankings can leave your ass tender for a couple of days. And even worse than standing, I hate the smug look on Colt's face every time he sees me wince when I sit down." Jenna's words were belied by the smirk on her face.

Selita raised her hands and began waving them dramatically before saying, "Those men, they think they are kings of the planet. They're always putting their hands on your asses, they are clunkers if they think I don't know because I do. And those two I raised, they always trying to get the bunny points with me, but I not playing that game. I know they just want me to not tell their mama they're taking an oar to their sweet woman. But I will be selling them to those gypsies that live up that river, you just see if I don't."

By the time Selita had finished her mini-tirade and turned back to her work, Bree, Kat, and Jenna were laughing so hard, they all had tears running down their cheeks. When Bree recovered enough to speak, she gasped out, "Oh my God, I really needed that laugh. She is the absolute best."

Jenna leaned over to pat Bree's shoulder and grinned. "We've had so much fun trying to decode her slaying of American sayings over the years, I can't even begin to tell you. It was always a lot more fun sorting it all out than trying to correct her. And seeing the baffled looks on my brothers' teammates' faces the first time they would visit? Priceless."

When the three of them had finally regained some sense of control over their giggling, Kat sighed, "We really did want to get you out of there for a couple of reasons, girlfriend. First of all, anyone who isn't 'one of them' usually has a low threshold for dealing with my loving husband's super-alpha self for very long, and that length of time is directly proportional to the number of his alpha pals that are in the room at the same time."

Jenna reached over and smacked her on the shoulder. "You are so getting your ass paddled if Alex hears you. And crap on a cracker, sister mine, you know the walls have eyes and ears in this freaking place since they took over. Hell, I'm betting the White House calls Colt and Mitch for surveillance tips."

"No, shit… oh damn and double damn, I forgot I'm not supposed to cuss. Anyway, we didn't want you to have to stay past what we consider the *saturation point* for most normal people. And… well, our motives aren't entirely altruistic, if you want the truth. We also wanted to talk to you about staying around after this mess is over. There seems to be a mini baby boom taking place in this area and—"

When Kat glanced at Jenna, Bree was certain her earlier guess had been right.

"Since it doesn't look like it's going to let up anytime soon, we could really use a good pediatrician. I hope you don't mind, but I mentioned to Doc Woods that I might know of someone who would be interested, and he practically begged me for your contact information. He's been trying to hand off that part of his practice for some time. Would you promise to at least think about it?"

Bree leaned in and in a conspiratorial whisper said, "Please don't tell any of the men, but Catherine has already called me about doing exactly that. I'd like very much to make my home here, but I need to see how it goes with Jamie and Ethan." She tried to keep the hopefulness from her tone but doubted she'd succeeded. "They haven't really said anything about wanting more than to teach me about the lifestyle, and I don't want to push them into a relationship they don't want. They are wonderful, and quite frankly, they deserve better than me." Deciding it was time to change the direction of the conversation, she quickly went on, "I'd like to go into town and look at the little dress shop I saw when I drove through. Who's in the mood for a little retail therapy?"

"Hot damn! I'm in! Kat, can you get the nanny to stay over for an hour or so? I have a few things I need to pick up as well... oddly enough, none of my clothes seem to be fitting just right anymore." Giggling like schoolgirls, they all agreed to meet out front in fifteen minutes. Kat called the garage to request someone bring up her SUV, so they'd have plenty of room for their purchases.

They scattered in three different directions, so they could grab what they'd need for their impromptu shopping excursion. Bree felt a cold chill race up her spine and the hair on the back of her neck straight stood up, but she dismissed the feeling that something bad was looming over her. Climax was a small town, but what were the odds she'd run into her parents or Hiram at the little boutique?

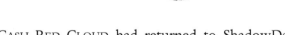

CASH RED CLOUD had returned to ShadowDance a few days ago. His last mission had been a cluster-fuck from the get-go, and he was looking forward to a little playtime at The Club after his shift in the Crow's Nest. When he'd caught pieces of the three subs' conversation in the kitchen, he'd texted all of their Doms. He was certain the men would monitor the situation closely, but just in case, he called the garage and put a stall order on the SUV. Sending a quick text to Alex, he updated him on the planned shopping trip, and his bosses one-word reply had made him chuckle. If he was a betting man, he'd put his money on there being some very sore asses at dinner tonight.

He let Alex know the vehicle request was on hold, and the women had evidently contacted Rissa Grayson because she had quickly closed her small spa in The Club and was making her way in the back door of the mansion. *Holy shit, this might be an interesting shift after all.*

Alex had replied his thanks, and Cash watched as six Doms stormed out the front door of the mansion to wait on their wayward subs. He'd wondered about Bryant Davis's location and with a few quick clicks discovered the bridge engineer was expected back from Denver at any minute. Oh, yes indeed, it was going to be an interesting shift for sure.

Davis was the only one of the Doms at ShadowDance who was even close to being as strict and hardline a Dom as Cash and his younger brother Collin. Since most of the Doms at ShadowDance were more lenient, the three of them had always enjoyed comparing notes. When they'd shared a training class for Doms, he and Bryant Davis had discovered a mutual preference for the edgier end of the play spectrum. It was going to be fun to watch his friend's reaction to his pregnant sub's plan to go on an unauthorized shopping trip. Cash didn't doubt for a minute the weary traveler would come up with some creative ways to punish his sub without causing any harm to their growing child. Smiling to himself, he couldn't help the wave of anticipation that washed through him. Damn, he was glad to be back home.

Chapter 24

BRYANT PULLED UP in front of the mansion to find the front entrance lined with pissed-off Doms. Just as he cleared the gate, Cash had sent him a text saying to join them at the front for the fireworks display, but he hadn't elaborated. It didn't take long for the others to bring him up to speed, and even though Rissa hadn't been privy to the reasons this trip was a train wreck looking for a place to happen, didn't mean his sweet wife wasn't in just as much hot water as the other women. Each of their sweet subs knew better than to leave the mountain without letting their men know where they were going and from the sounds of things, Bree had been the ringleader this time.

The fact it wasn't Kat or Jenna surprised him, hell, it seemed to surprise everyone. Oh indeed, it looked like the subs were inadvertently getting ready to throw a hell of a welcome home party for both he and Cash. There was nothing like a few great punishment scenes to make a Dom feel welcomed back into the fold.

Just as the women came barreling out the front door, he heard their collective gasp at the sight of the men gathered there, but it was Rissa's high-pitched squeal of delight that stood out. He was ready when she launched herself into his arms and started kissing his eyes, forehead, and cheeks before finally plunging her sweet tongue deeply into his mouth. He had to consciously hold himself back because the urge to strip her naked and plunge balls-deep into her warmth right here on the front steps was almost more than he could resist.

He noticed although his beautiful wife was quite a lot "rounder" than when he'd left a week ago, she felt lighter. They'd be having a discussion about her continued insecurity about her weight as soon as he got her alone. He'd be willing to bet she was lying through her teeth to Mitch about what she was eating, and since she'd learned to block Grayson's psychic gifts, she'd been regularly blindsiding them both.

Alex leaned over to Zach and groaned he was worried he would be permanently deaf from the high-pitched scream Rissa let out as soon as she'd seen Bryant. But his hearing had evidently returned quickly because he'd practically growled when he heard Katarina's softly spoken, "Oh shit," just as she crossed the threshold and saw them all assembled outside.

ETHAN LAUGHED TO himself. Seeing Alex Lamont standing with his legs shoulder-width apart and his arms crossed over his chest like the others would have been intimidating as hell to each and every sub in The Club. Katarina had taken one look at her husband's body language and known she was in more trouble than she was going to be able to talk her way out of this time.

Ethan had heard Alex complaining they'd gotten too lax with Kat and she was back to taking risks with her safety. In his opinion, she was probably looking for reassurance her husbands still cared enough to take her in hand, but he wasn't one to tell another Dom how to handle their submissive. What Kat didn't realize was that on this point, Alex and Zach would always take a hard line.

Alex had warned her time and again she was to protect herself and their children above all else. Watching her face pale, it was clear she fucking knew better than this shit and both of her husbands were about to blow a gasket. When Kat started to take a step back, Zach leaned forward.

"Don't you dare move, kitten. You are in deep—very, very deep. Don't compound the problem by trying to step away from us."

Colt wrapped his hand around Jenna's wrist, and Ethan didn't hear what she said, but Colt turned four shades of red, and Ethan was waiting to see steam come out of the man's ears. *Jesus Christ, Jenna, use that genius IQ of yours to control your mouth.*

Just as he and Jamie started to approach Bree, he heard the alarms of each of their phones go off simultaneously. Whatever had happened, it was big. They didn't even take time to check their phones before they began herding the wayward women back inside. They had just gotten everyone turned when he heard the first rifle shot whiz by and watched in horror as it landed close enough to Bree to send concrete chips spraying against her bare legs. Seeing the blood running down both of her calves had been just the catalyst the women needed to scramble for the safety of the house.

The next shot hit Bree in the shoulder exactly where the chip had been. The shooter was trying to make sure the chip was destroyed. Unfortunately, the fucker with the rifle bead on Bree didn't know the damned thing had already been removed and downloaded. Evidently, all the interested parties hadn't gotten the fucking memo that the chip was on its way to Guatemala. Ethan watched as Alex slipped his hand into his pocket and retrieved his earbud com unit slipped it into place. Tapping it once before snarling, "Talk to me."

Ethan knew Alex's team would already be using the trajectory- and sound-tracing software Mitch Grayson had developed to determine the shooter's location, but he wanted to find out if anyone in the Crow's Nest had a visual on the bastard. When Zach handed him an earbud, Ethan heard Cash's voice as he responded to the questions Alex was firing at him.

"We're on it, boss. He's on the southern ledge of Meadow Ridge. I've got cameras on him, but he's a pro—all dressed for the Black Magic Dance of Death. You take care of the women, I've already sent a call to EMS and local law enforcement, ETA three minutes. I've reviewed the tape and know exactly where the other shot went. I've got a guy headed down there now to mark the bullets."

Cash's pregnant pause got Ethan's attention.

"Fuck, the first wave of response just breached the ridge and met two vehicles leaving the scene. Both were moving at high rates of speed and driven by men. There's a dead woman up there. I'll advise as soon as I have more." Ethan continued to cradle Bree in his arms, but he could see Jamie's torn expression. Ordinarily, Jamie Creed would be scrambling toward whatever weapon he had stashed closest. Ethan saw Alex quickly nod toward his friend and woman. Ethan saw the relief that flooded Jamie's expression. They all knew that if that had been Katarina, Alex wouldn't have wanted to be anywhere but at her side, so he'd understood Jamie's reluctance to give chase.

Ethan was glad he'd already had his arm wrapped

around Bree, so it had been easy to catch her before she'd hit the ground. He continued to carry her as they followed Zach who was barking orders and leading them up to the mansion's safe rooms. The nursery was already in lockdown, and the only other two designated safe rooms on the second floor were the master suite and the smaller suite he and Creed had been sharing with Bree.

Zach directed him to Bree's suite and moved the others to the larger rooms of the master suite at the end of the hall. Zach and Creed had both been trained as medics and as soon as Zach returned with his med-bag the two had fallen into a well-choreographed routine. Ethan sent up a silent prayer of gratitude his friend had been cross-trained as a medic as he watched him work on their woman. And even though he knew she wasn't in any mortal danger, he was still scared out of his mind for her. When Bree looked up at him with confusion in her eyes, Ethan tried to distract her.

"Did you know many snipers are cross-trained as medics because their positions are so often far removed from their teammates?" He didn't bother to tell her the narrative was a necessary distraction because he suddenly felt as if all the blood was draining from his brain. Zach glanced up and his raised eyebrow was all it took for Ethan to find a chair before he woke up on the floor.

Through the black dots that were clouding his vision, he saw Zach's relieved expression and heard him say, "Cash was right, it's a through and through," telling Ethan the injury wasn't nearly as bad as it could have been, but damned if he was still trying to pull in a deep breath.

Jesus, Jantz, get a fucking grip. You're a damned sniper, for Christ's sake. You never batted an eye at the sight of the damage a rifle shot did before, so what's your problem?

Even as he asked himself the question, he already knew the answer—none of those people had been the woman he was in love with. And just that quickly, the truth he'd been dancing around since he'd first laid eyes on Bree was staring him right in the face. He loved her with everything in him. The thought that Cash had told them she'd expressed insecurity about his and Creed's intentions, not more than an hour ago, tore at his heart. They would be remedying that misunderstanding immediately. When he heard the knock at the door, he moved close but didn't release the locks until he'd gotten confirmation EMS had arrived and waited on the other side of the secured door.

Ethan watched as Jamie stepped back and let Zach and the paramedics work. Ethan understood his need for a minute to shift modes and knew his friend and long-time teammate was probably already feeling the adrenaline rush starting to ebb. It was something every soldier was trained to recognize and cope with, but there wasn't any doubt in his mind, this one was going to be the mother of all crashes for both of them.

Watching as the paramedics and Zach prepared to lift Bree onto the gurney for transport, he was shocked when she'd reached for him and Jamie, then burst into tears. Hell, she'd held it together through the most painful parts and now she was sobbing? *What the hell?* When she finally managed to speak, the only words she managed to choke out were, "Please don't leave me there."

Ethan heard Zach's end of the conversation with the physician on duty at the local hospital and wasn't surprised to see him reach into his bag and withdraw a small prefilled syringe. When he'd squeezed the contents into the IV the paramedics had started, Bree went instantly still, and the eerie silence sent a chill down Ethan's spine.

Jamie told him the sedative Zach had given her was authorized, necessary, and in her best interest, but it still nearly tore his heart out to think her last thoughts had been the stark terror they weren't going to be right by her side.

He and Jamie flanked the gurney as it was rolled down the long hall. They would make sure at least one of them rode in the ambulance with her. When Jamie had pointed to his blood-covered clothing, he was shocked to see it covered in Bree's blood. Waving Creed on, Ethan opted to clean up before heading to the hospital in his truck.

Taking a quick shower, he was almost to his truck when Colt stepped up and handed him a small holster and two clips. Christ, he'd been so focused on getting Bree to the hospital, he'd forgotten his first objective should have been her safety. As if his former team leader had read his thoughts, Colt shook his head, then leveled him with a look filled with compassion.

"She'll be okay and so will you and Creed. Don't worry about forgetting this, let that thought go and be vigilant from now on." Ethan knew his doubt had reflected in his expression when Colt added, "Hey, man, it's difficult to remember your original objective was to drain the swamp when you're up to your ass in alligators." Ethan couldn't help but smile and knew his relief had shown when Colt nodded once and turned on his heel, heading back into the house.

An hour later, Ethan found himself surrounded by the friends he considered his second family, and was grateful beyond measure for their support. He thought back to Colt's words and realized that moment had been a perfect example of why Colt Matthews had been an incredibly successful team leader. Hell, their Division Commander had admitted to having an unofficial "waiting list" of guys wanting on Colt's team. The man's ability to bring out the best in his team was legendary, and today, he'd recognized Ethan was dancing on the edge and had gently tugged him back onto solid ground.

There wasn't any question about whether Bree would be alright, but their friends gathered in the waiting room because that's what friends do. Ethan didn't know whether Bree would be thrilled or overwhelmed by their kindness. There wasn't any doubt in his mind Jamie had been right when he'd said once that Climax, Colorado was second only to the bayou when it came to feelings of kinship.

When he entered the crowded room, he moved toward Jamie and saw his best friend try to give him a reassuring smile. "She's going to be fine. They are just stitching her up, then we'll be able to get her out of here."

Ethan hadn't realized how worried he'd been until he'd heard Jamie's reassuring words. Feeling like the huge breath he let out drained some of the apprehension he'd been feeling was a relief, but there was still something niggling in the back of his mind, telling him the other shoe was about to drop, and that was a feeling no well-trained soldier ever ignored.

Looking around the room he noted that there were only a few people he didn't recognize and only one who seemed totally out of place. A man who appeared to be in his early-to-mid-fifties leaned casually against the wall close to the door. There was something vaguely familiar about the man, but his hat was pulled so low in the front, Ethan wasn't able to get a good look at his face. Just as Ethan started toward the stranger, Doc Woods stormed into the room.

"Damn, you guys are an embarrassment to Doms everywhere. Can't you take better care of your women? I'm getting mighty tired of patching them back up because you yo-yos were playing Tiddlywinks instead of being SEALs. Hell, it's no wonder this country is in such a sorry state."

The old doctor might have really sounded like a pain in the ass, but his wink toward the women was a dead giveaway he'd been joking. When Doc continued, his voice had switched to the seasoned professional that he was.

"Now, we've given that pretty lady enough *happy meds* you aren't going to be able to rely on her for the medical history information I need. Do any of you know if she is allergic to anything? I'm particularly interested in allergies to antibiotics—penicillin or sulfa drugs to be specific." It must have been obvious from the blank stares he was receiving, no one in the room knew, and Ethan watched the old doctor turn to leave the room, shaking his head and muttering words he was sure were best left unheard. When Doc reached the door, the stranger reached out and grasped his arm.

"She is very allergic to penicillin. Don't even touch her with it." At that point, all hell broke loose in the waiting room, but Doc hustled the elderly man out into the hall before anyone could get to him. When Dylan Marshall stepped into the doorway, blocking Ethan and Jamie's exit, Ethan fought the urge to growl at his friend to move his ass out of their way.

"What the fuck is this about? Hell, you're going to wake up my wife and son, and they aren't even on this floor." He looked over at his young deputy and snapped, "Update me." The young man gave the sheriff a short but accurate account of things, and by the time he'd finished, and he and Jamie finally wedged themselves around the mammoth man, Doc and the stranger had already disappeared.

Chapter 25

ETHAN THREATENED, AND Jamie had tried to charm every nurse in sight, but they still hadn't been able to get any information about Bree's condition. Nobody was talking. Finally, Zach Lamont moved to the nurses' station, and after a short conversation with the head nurse, he led them both through a maze of rooms until they were standing in the doorway to Bree's room. Both men were struck speechless as they watched as the stranger held their woman in his arms, stroking her hair, and speaking softly to her as she sobbed.

Ethan could count on one hand the number of times he'd been totally speechless. Hell, he was a Jantz, he'd been taught to be ready for anything from the time he'd been in diapers. His family was as close to royalty as you could get in Texas. The oppressive pressure of that life had been what led him to seek the anonymity of military service. Ethan still believed he'd be forced to buckle under and return home at some point, but he was determined to enjoy his freedom as long as possible.

Duty would eventually call, and there would be no way to avoid it, but he damned well planned to delay it as long as possible. But no amount of social or military training had prepared him for the sound of Bree's broken-hearted sobs. Nor had anything taught him how to hold back his harsh tone.

"Who are you and what have you done to her?" The man's expression was filled with anguish, but he didn't move from where he sat.

"I am John Gillette, I am Sab—I mean, Bree's father. And may I ask who you are and why you are in my daughter's room?"

Ethan couldn't believe it. *This man is her father? Why is Bree crying, and if he was happy to see her, why the look of desolation?*

"Well, Mr. Gillette, Bree is a very special woman in our lives. I'm not going to lie to you, we'll be doing everything in our power to keep her here… with us. I'll make that clear right up front. I'm Ethan Jantz and that fella over there with the steam coming out of his ears because you are touching our woman is Jamie Creed."

The mention of their names seemed to bring Bree back to the moment, she looked up through tears. "Jamie? Ethan? Oh God, finally!" When she started to scramble from the bed, both he and Jamie hurried to her side. He saw her looking between her father and them, knowing she wouldn't miss the tension that was thick enough to cut with a knife.

"Please, it's important to me that you three get along. You are the most important people in the world to me, please. I've already lost my dad once, and I can't bear it again. And… well, he's just told me that my mom lost her life trying to keep Hiram from shooting me and—" Her words were cut off by more sobs.

Doc Woods stormed into the room—a man clearly on a mission. "If you three are going to upset my patient, I'm going to unleash Katarina on you, don't think I won't. She is in the waiting room and primed for a confrontation.

Judging by her reluctance to sit down, I'm fairly certain Alex and Zach are involved in her antagonistic attitude. Of course, their shit-eating grins are clues as well."

Ethan wanted to hug the elderly doctor because his words had done exactly as the old fart had intended. The smile that broke through Bree's grief was the sweetest thing he'd ever seen. She giggled when Doc waggled his eyebrows at her, and Ethan decided at that moment he was now the president of Doc's fan club.

"Well, now that's a much more pleasant expression, my dear. Let me get these jokers out of here. You and I are going to have a brief chat before we release you." With that, he opened the door and shooed the men out into the hall. Turning back to her, he said, "Now, I understand that you have had one hell of a day. I know you still have some challenges to get off your plate before you are really free to make a commitment, but I want you to give some serious consideration to making Climax your home." The man had obviously seen her startled expression and smiled kindly at her.

"Dear, you need to realize this is a small town, and this hospital is underwritten by the Lamont family. I had a nice long chat with one of my dearest friends yesterday, and Catherine assures me that your medical license will be back in place in a matter of days or a couple of weeks at the longest. She also told me she holds you in the highest regard. I have to tell you as recommendations go, they don't get any better than that, in my humble opinion."

Bree was stunned. Oh, she was flattered, too, no doubt

about it, but even she realized that she'd had too many meds to make a decision right now. But now that she thought about it, she realized he hadn't asked her to decide, he'd just requested she give it careful consideration. Even without the drugs, she wouldn't be able to make a commitment after just learning she'd lost her mom. She had no idea how long her father would be tied up with the legal system, and she still didn't know exactly where she stood with Jamie and Ethan.

Sighing to herself, she just nodded her head and quietly agree to consider it. "I promise I'll think it over. To be honest, I love it here, but there are a lot of things that I need to work through before I can really make a decision. Can I let you know later?"

"Honey, I've been handling things here alone for years, so a few more weeks isn't going to break me. But as you may or may not know, Rissa is my granddaughter, and I'd rather not deliver her baby because it just doesn't seem right. Not to mention, I'm fairly certain I wouldn't be able to make an unemotional decision if anything went wrong. God, I love that girl." The wistful expression on his face warmed her heart, and at that moment, Bree knew there wasn't any other place she'd rather be… no other doctor she'd rather work with. She and Doc Woods were going to become fast friends.

Chapter 26

AFTER CHECKING IN on Mia and baby Nathanial, Katarina Lamont stormed into the waiting room, and there was no question in anyone's mind the diminutive sub was on a mission. There wasn't anything submissive in her body language. Kat was pissed and wasn't making any effort to conceal it.

"How is she? When is she being released? What time did Doc get here? Is he still with her? Ethan, who is that man I saw you and Jamie talking to in the hall? Where is Jenna? Isn't she here? What's taking them so damned long? Geez, doesn't anyone in here see me? Am I invisible or something? Damn and double damn this is really turning out to be a pissy day."

"Katarina, language." Alex's tone held a stern warning that for once his wife seemed to listen to. When she winced, Alex stepped forward and spoke quietly in her ear. Ethan watched as the tiny woman settled immediately, then lean into Alex's chest. Alex hugged her before setting her back enough he could look into her face as he answered her litany of questions.

"Bree is fine. She is going to be dismissed soon, and we'll have her back at ShadowDance within the hour. Doc was here waiting for her when the ambulance arrived, and yes, he is still with her. Ethan can answer for himself about the man he and Jamie were speaking to. As for Jenna and Colt, they are still at home. It seems Jenna isn't feeling well. You wouldn't know anything about that would you?" At his raised eyebrow Kat turned crimson.

Zach leaned forward and said, "Kitten? Now is not a good time for you to be holding back information from us. The ice you're skating on is still mighty thin."

Ethan had always loved watching Zach Lamont work his magic with submissives. While Alex was known to take the straight path with subs, Zach was the Master of Charm. His natural ability to convince a sub to put herself in his hands was a skill every Dom Ethan knew envied.

He spent enough time at the mansion to know Alex's personality mirrored their mother's "run to the roar" worldview. But Zach was much more like their father. Daniel Lamont was a brilliant businessman whose business acumen was only eclipsed by his people skills. Ethan had met Daniel before he'd met his sons. He'd been waiting outside his father's office in Dallas one afternoon before leaving for BUDS training when Daniel stepped from behind the closed door. They'd been introduced, and when the elder Lamont learned he was leaving for BUDS, he'd given him a business card with a quickly scribbled note in Latin and said to show it to his sons if they happened to meet.

Of course, he'd spent enough time in boarding school to have learned Latin, so the note had been easy to read, and Ethan remembered laughing out loud when he'd read it. *"A man of integrity, deal well with him but never his father who is an ass."*

He still carried the card in his wallet all these years later. As it happened, he had met the Lamont brothers on a mission several years later, and they had all enjoyed a laugh about the card. Even though they'd all laughed, the influence those few words hastily scribbled on the back of a small rectangular piece of card stock had on Alex and Zach had been unmistakable.

Kat's stuttering brought Ethan back to the moment, and he smiled as he watched her try to figure out a way to avoid answering the question. Zach leaned against the wall, watching her struggle between compliance and loyalty to her best friend and sister-in-law. When Ethan glanced at Alex, he saw he was struggling not to laugh at his wife's obvious unease.

Zach finally broke the silence by reminding her lying by omission was a punishable offense, just like out-and-out deception or attempting to leave the mountain without letting someone know her plans. That had obviously been all the incentive she'd needed because she finally dropped her chin and whispered, "But I promised not to tell. Please don't make me break my promise."

Ethan had been relieved when Zach wrapped his arms around her and held her close. "Kitten, we already know Jenna is pregnant, but I have to tell you, both Alex and I have the utmost respect for your loyalty. As long as it is used appropriately, we'll never demand you break a confidence. But rest assured, if it is ever a question of someone's safety, you better sing like a canary, understood?" When Kat nodded, Zach nodded, "Good enough. Now, I believe you had a question for Ethan."

Smiling at the tiny woman, Ethan explained what he had learned and thanked her for her friendship with Bree. Jamie joined them and leaned down to speak directly to the petite woman.

"Sweetness, if you could see your way to help us convince Bree to stay in Climax after all this is resolved, we'd surely be indebted to you. Hell, we might even be persuaded to sponsor one of those weekend shopping expeditions you are always trying to find an escort for." When he winked at her, Ethan wanted to roll his eyes at his friend's corny line. When she blushed and ducked her head like a smitten schoolgirl, he groaned aloud as laughter filled the room.

Doc Woods walked in before Kat could respond, but Ethan was sure Jamie's words had already met their mark. Doc looked at both he and Jamie as he shook his head.

"That wicked witch we call a head nurse is helping your sweet woman into some clothes and then she's free to go," Doc studied them both for long seconds before continuing. "I'm gonna tell you straight up, I'm trying to talk her into staying after all this nonsense blows over, and I'd appreciate it if you two wouldn't muck it up for me." Then he turned to Kat. "My dear, you look radiant. Are these two treating you right? If not, you just let me know, and I'm sure I could make time to have a chat with their mama."

Alex stepped forward and shook Doc's hand. "Don't be putting thoughts in her head that are just going to get her in more trouble, Doc. Since you've recognized the problem with Nurse Ratched, I'll leave you to it. Personally, I think her communication skills are deplorable. Now, let's get these two headed back to Bree, and the rest of us will clear out." Turning back to look down at Kat, his expression softened, and Ethan knew both Alex and Zach would be showing her just how much they valued her submission.

"Come, my love, Zach and I have plans for you." When she started to speak, he stilled her with a hand and the continued, "Yes, Love, I know you want to set things up for Bree's return, and we plan to help you with that, but after that's finished, you are all ours."

Had Ethan not been standing so close he wouldn't have heard Zach's softly whispered words.

"Look around you, kitten, every Dom in the room is watching. Alex's thinly veiled promise to fuck you seven ways to Sunday has every one of them sporting wood and anxiously anticipating getting their own sub naked." Kat's soft gasp made Ethan want to kick Zach's ass. How the hell was he supposed to walk down the hall past Bree's father with a hard-on the size of Texas? *Fucker did it on purpose, too, count on it.*

Chapter 27

Bree was struggling to get the shirt over her head, and her shoulder was throbbing like a bitch. *Why didn't I just let that wicked woman help me? Crap on a cracker—what was her boggle, anyway? She has to be the crabbiest woman I've ever met.* Deciding she didn't have any choice but to call for help, Bree was thrilled when Rissa stepped through the curtain surrounding the small treatment room. Her new friend rushed to Bree's side and snickered.

"Having trouble there, girlfriend? Need a hand?"

"Oh, Rissa, you have no idea how happy I am to see you. I really didn't want to have to call that nurse back. God, that woman is beyond wicked." Bree was relieved to have gotten her arms untangled and threaded through the sleeves of the baggy scrubs she'd been given. Standing up and seeing herself in the mirror caused her to groan. "Shit! I look like something the cat dragged in... no, I look like something the cat would refuse to be seen dragging home."

"Sit down, and I'll work you over while we talk because those men of yours are sure to storm this place soon."

"How did you get in here? Oh Lord, are you okay? You aren't having problems with your pregnancy from all this are you?" Bree knew she hadn't been able to hide the panic in her voice, but she didn't care.

"God Lord Almighty, girl, what's wrong with you? I'm in fine shape... hell, round's a shape isn't it?" They both laughed, then Rissa leaned closer and said, "I just wanted to let you know I have a house you can use if you decide to stay in Climax. I'd be thrilled to have you live in it. It belonged to my Granny and well, you see, it's a long story but the short version is Mitch bought it in my name when I was forced to let it go a while back. I love the place too much to part with it, so I'm going to rent it out. The condo Mitch and Bryant had when we got married is much nicer and larger, so we'll be staying there. Now that I've spit out so much info, you're likely thinking I'm Queen Quacks A-Lot. I just want you to know I'd sure love to have you stick around. You're funny and smart, and those two men of yours are crazy about you. Oh, and I'd sure love to have another doc around in case this baby decides to make a surprise appearance, and I don't have time to get to my obstetrician. And Lord, I don't want Doc Woods looking at my hoo-ha now that I've found out he's my granddad. It's just wrong, ya know what I mean?"

By the time Rissa had finished Bree was shaking with laughter. "Oh my God, you are so good for my soul. And thank you for the offer of the house. I haven't made a final decision yet, but I honestly can't imagine leaving. There are some things I need to check on and work out, but... well, please don't offer it to anyone else just yet, okay?"

Rissa clapped her hands in delight and whispered, "Oh. Honey, I'm so happy to hear that, and I promise to keep it to myself... well, mostly. You know I have to tell Kat and Jenna, or they'd have my hide. But those men of yours? They're on their own. Now, I better get back out to that waiting room before I find myself in as much trouble as

Kat, and oh, sister, that must have been ugly because Kat hasn't sat down since they got here!" When Bree's eyes went wide, she continued, "Oh don't you worry, Alex and Zach wouldn't ever actually hurt her, but they surely would paddle her sweet ass, and I'm sure they did. But likely the worst of it was they didn't let her come. See you soon and welcome to the neighborhood… in advance." She laughed as she made her way through the curtain.

JAMIE WAS SURE Rissa had seen them walk up to the curtain, then back away. She'd have known they were listening to her conversation with Bree, so he wasn't surprised to see her sly smile as she walked by and gave them each a fist bump. She'd be getting a nice big basket of flowers and some very special baby gifts. He'd always liked Rissa, but right now, he wanted to hug her until she squeaked.

"Thanks, sweet cheeks. We owe you—big time. We won't forget this, I promise you."

Rissa just smiled and teased, "Don't you be telling anyone I did something nice. I have a reputation to maintain, you know." She kept walking, and they turned back toward the curtained divider. Nodding to each other, they both knew it was time to make sure their woman knew precisely what their intentions were.

Chapter 28

Lying back, soaking up the warm sunshine and listening to the soft lapping of the nearby pool, Bree thought back over the two weeks since she'd lost her mother. Her father had been hustled away by Homeland Security before she'd even been released from the hospital, but at least he was being allowed to keep in touch with her, and from the way things were shaping up, he might very well be returning to Colorado within the next month or two.

Truthfully, he really didn't have much information, her mom had clearly been the one involved in the arms and information brokering over the years. Finding out the depth of Christina Gillette's betrayal had left both Bree and her dad totally shell-shocked. She hoped he would eventually move closer to her, so they could help each other heal.

The gunshot wound to her shoulder had healed faster than expected, and she was even starting some lightweight training as physical therapy, so her strength was rebounding quickly. The only thing that was missing was sex.

Bree was about to climb the walls. Ethan and Jamie were smothering her and not in a good way. She felt like a kid who had been given this wonderful new toy to play with for a few days, only to have it taken away from her the first time she had the least little health problem. Rolling to her side and propping her head on her hand, she directed her question to Kat and Rissa who were dangling their feet in the pool in front of the waterfall.

"You have both been injured since you became a sub, right?"

"Oh yeah," Kat snorted, "and you don't even have to tell us what's bugging you because we already know. Hell, this was the hot topic of conversation in the spa yesterday after you left." Both women giggled, and Bree was starting to get annoyed before Kat finally continued. "Don't get your panties in a twist, sister. It wasn't a bad thing, we could just tell you were edgy and since we've 'been there, done that,' there wasn't any question about the cause. You aren't getting laid."

Bree knew her mouth had dropped open, but she couldn't help it. The women she'd made friends with since coming to ShadowDance never ceased to amaze her with the casual way they spoke about sex. Kat turned to Rissa and waved her hand in Bree's direction.

"Look at her. Jesus Christ on a crutch, she still does that guppy imitation when we talk about sex—and she's a doctor for f... anny's sake. Good Lord, wouldn't you think she'd be used to us by now. No matter, she'll catch on eventually... maybe, well I hope so... damn... anyway, as I was saying, we know what you are going through and can only tell you that you'll have to figure it out and soon, or your head is going to start spinning around on your shoulders."

By the time Kat was finished, Rissa was holding her very round baby bump and laughing so hard, she had tears streaming down her cheeks. It hadn't escaped Bree's attention that Rissa was gaining weight at a much healthier rate since Bryant had returned home. She knew he was the stricter of Rissa's two dominant husbands, and he'd been upset when he'd learned how little his wife had gained while he'd been finishing up a bridge project out of the country.

"Well, thanks so much for the fortune cookie advice there, sweet friend. Crap, that doesn't help me at all. You were supposed to tell me how to get sex, not give me some watered-down version of 'figure it out and stop whining.'" Blowing out her breath, she finally asked, "Do you think you could get me into The Club tonight? I've been dying to see what it's like when the members are there, and if I'm not getting any action, I ought to at least get to enjoy it vicariously."

Rissa gasped and started shaking her head vigorously before gathering up her stuff and hot-footing it out of there. As she left, Bree heard her saying something about not going down for this one as she rounded the corner. Staring after her, Bree was shocked by her reaction, and it was only Kat's bark of laughter that refocused her attention on her hostess.

"Holy shit, I never thought I'd live to see the day when Rissa would tuck tail and run at the thought of getting a nice satisfying paddling. Boy oh boy, Bryant's head is going to grow two sizes overnight, you just watch and see if I'm not right. Damn and double damn—this is a real dilemma. I know where you are coming from, I really do, but I have to tell you, sneaking into The Club is beyond what even I am willing to risk. I suggest you reconsider that option. Give me a day or so to come up with something else because sneaking in there will be painful for you and embarrassing too. Don't get me wrong, I enjoy an erotic spanking or a well-handled flogger as much as anyone, but I don't want to be displayed and punished as an example to all the members either." She shuddered, then looked over at Bree.

"Okay let me tell you what happened to me... *once*. I was in sitting at the bar in The Club's largest lounge area, chatting up one of the subs who helps out serving drinks, etcetera." Running her hand nervously through her hair, she finally took a deep breath and released it slowly before continuing. "Anyway, this jackass Dom from back east comes in and quacks out his order like he's the king duck or something. His behavior was incredibly rude, and I told him so. Well, that brought a shit storm my way in a big hurry.

"Alex put me in the stocks, ripped my pretty dress, so my bare ass was exposed to the world, then put a sign up that said, 'Bratty and Mouthy—Needs Guidance—2 Free Swats per Dom'. Then he stood by and watched every Dom in the place, well almost every one, smack me with the damned wooden paddle he'd chosen. I was in those stupid stocks for over an hour, and I didn't sit for several days.

"My ass and thighs turned the most amazing shade of purple... before they turned a nasty yellow-green. That was the only time I was tempted to give up being a sub. I was mortified, not from the paddling, but because I'd embarrassed Alex and Zach. They are the owners of this wonderful and well-respected BDSM club, and I felt that as their sub, I was a total loser."

Bree was shocked to see the tear that trailed down Kat's cheek. She wouldn't have been surprised if the woman had wanted to quit because of the paddling and bruises, but her admission she'd considered walking away from the lifestyle because she'd failed to live up to what she considered her husbands' exacting standards shocked her.

"Did they say they were disappointed in you?"

"Well, sort of... oh hell. They said they knew I was better than that, and they expected me to be a good example and not embarrass them. I cried for days. I was heartbroken to think I'd let them down. I know I come off as this catty, confident woman, but the only thing I have ever wanted was a family and a husband that loved me as much as I loved him. Well, I got a bonus and got the two men I'd loved since forever and three gorgeous children, but I still felt like the stuff beneath pond scum."

Bree was really surprised because even though she'd read stories about how much subs thrived on pleasing others, she'd still felt as if she was the only one to have fallen so deeply in love that pleasing the two men in her life was quickly becoming an obsession, and that scared the soup out of her.

"I can't believe they didn't try to make it up to you or at least explain things. Are their expectations really that unreasonably high?"

"Oh God, no! They didn't know how devastating it was to me emotionally. I couldn't tell them because it would have just been another epic fail on my part. No, I just sucked it up, and I've really tried to stay away from The Club as much as I can since then. I know it's cowardly, but I'd just die a thousand deaths if I messed up again. Anyway, I only started this pity party so you'd see why I don't want to help you sneak into The Club. It really would be a huge problem for Alex and Zach, and I promise you, they would find out I'd helped you. Hell, I'm hoping splashing my feet has covered up enough of this conversation, I'm already in deep shit."

"Katarina, language." Alex's voice boomed from a few feet behind them, and Bree was so startled she nearly launched herself out of the lounge chair. "Love, I believe we need to have a chat." Then he turned toward Bree and said, "Bree, your men are also on their way. Before they get here, let me give you a bit of advice."

Oh shit, Bree, you've done it now. Not only have you gotten Kat in deep, but you are going to sink like a stone on this one.

Once he knew she was focused on him again, she saw Alex nod once before he continued. "Bree, the only time you will truly disappoint your Doms will be when you don't trust them enough to share the truth of your feelings. Behavior can be corrected, usually quite easily, but trust is built over time, and it's precious. Don't assume they know what you are thinking or that what you are feeling isn't important to them because I assure you, a true Dom's entire reason for being is to take care of his greatest treasure, and that's the submissive in his care."

Zach stepped around the corner and held out his hand to Kat, and when she went to him, he wrapped his arms around her. "Kitten, we have arranged for the children to spend the night with Colt and Jenna. We want to spend some time with you, this issue is too important for us to ignore. Listen to what your Master is saying to Bree because he is also speaking to you."

Alex returned his gaze to Bree. "Without trust, no Ds relationship can survive. You have to be honest with them, and that requires you to be honest with yourself as well." He looked deeply into her eyes, watching her for several agonizing seconds. "Follow your heart, Bree. If you truly listen to the words it speaks to you, you'll always find your way."

Chapter 29

BREE WATCHED THE Lamonts walk away and was struck by how much she envied the trio. She didn't care about their wealth or material possessions, but she had always craved a love like theirs. To have one man who loved you with that intensity would have been a blessing, but she had two within her grasp if she was just brave enough to reach out to them.

It was suddenly clear to her that Jamie and Ethan had been waiting for her to be emotionally ready for everything being with them would entail. After she'd gotten out of the hospital, they'd patiently explained exactly what they wanted in terms of a relationship and emphasized they were willing to wait until she was healed enough to make a decision.

At the time, their words had annoyed the hell out of her, after all, it was her shoulder that was injured, not her mind. Before this moment, their words had sounded hollow, but now, she could see how considerate they'd been. After speaking to Kat and having Alex's words hit her directly in the heart, she was stunned by how accurate her men's assessment had been.

Trust was the one thing she hadn't been able to freely give anyone since her kidnapping. Everything she'd thought she knew about herself and her family had been blown apart, and now, it was heartbreakingly clear she hadn't really given Jamie or Ethan her trust. It would be a leap of faith, but she knew anything worth having was worth working for. *Nothing ventured, nothing gained.*

She wasn't sure how long she'd been standing there, lost in her own thoughts and self-analysis, but when she turned to pick up her things, she came face-to-face with both of the men she'd discovered owned her heart.

"Oh! I was just getting ready to come and find you. Um... I want to apologize to you both." She felt tears burn in her eyes, and suddenly, she wasn't as confident as she'd been just a few seconds earlier.

JAMIE HAD BEEN in the gym working out when Ethan called from the Crow's Nest and said he was patching something through to the nearest monitor. As he'd watched and listened to everything play out in the gardens, he'd been touched by Alex's attempt to open Bree's heart, and in Jamie's opinion, his friend and boss had hit the problem dead center.

The look of self-realization on Bree's face had lightened his heart. Damn, this past two weeks had been absolute torture. He and Ethan had known she needed to heal—both physically and emotionally, but they'd started to wonder if their love would ever be enough. He'd always believed love could conquer almost anything, but her scars were soul deep.

Just last night, his *grand-mère* called, and he'd shaken his head and chuckled when her name popped up on the screen. The woman's timing was always remarkable.

When he'd answered, she'd simply said, "The time is now," and hung up. Perhaps today's events shouldn't be all that shocking. God, he loved that old woman. He and Ethan were already planning a trip to introduce Bree to their families, just as soon as they got a ring on her finger.

Jamie left the gym and moved quickly to the gardens, arriving at the same time Ethan stepped into the enclosure. They stood for several minutes, watching their beautiful sub stand beside the waterfall, lost in thought. They let her work it through until it looked as if a weight had lifted from her small shoulders, and she took a deep breath before turning to find them watching her.

When she said she'd been on her way to find them, he and Ethan both froze. Could they have misinterpreted? Finally, the word *apologize* penetrated the fog of confusion, and he wondered what the hell she could possibly have to apologize for. Jamie looked at Ethan, whose puzzled expression mirrored his own baffled feeling. Jamie stepped forward and took her hand in his.

"Bree, let's sit down and talk for a minute, then we need to move this discussion someplace much more private."

"Okay, but please let me tell you about what I've just learned." Once they'd all sat down, she leaned forward and looked directly at each of them before sighing. "I'm sorry it took me so long to be ready... well, ready to be honest about trusting again. Honestly, I have trusted you from that first day, but my spirit was so tattered, I wasn't strong enough to recognize what was so clearly the truth. But my worry is that I... well, that I won't be enough." When she saw they were going to protest, she forged ahead.

"No, please let me explain. I know you are both very experienced. From what I've been able to gather, you are popular and sought-after Doms at The Club. I really don't know if I'll ever be any good at being a submissive.

"I had to let go of so much of what I considered *me* when I entered the witness protection program, I'm still struggling to put it all together. It's hard to change everything about you and suddenly become another person. I'm still trying to figure out who Bree is, but I know she trusts you with everything she is, and well, if you are still interested in teaching her, I mean me, about submission, well..."

Jamie noticed she had let her words trail off because they both had huge smiles on their faces. She wasn't sure if they were laughing at her inept explanation or if they were sincerely pleased by her words, but she didn't seem to care. Seeing Bree smile at their reaction was enough to melt Jamie's heart.

ETHAN LEANED FORWARD to grasp her small hand in his, drawing lazy circles over her palm for long seconds. He kept his gaze focused on her beautiful face as a play of emotions moved over her expression. It was easy to see she was struggling and unsure what they expected, but it was important for them to give her a minute to work things out in her mind. They'd learned one of the ways her brilliant mind worked was to sort things into small, manageable bits of information, so she didn't feel overwhelmed by the onslaught. Years of minimal sensory input as a result of living in remote locations had left its mark on her. The only exception they'd seen was when she'd been in professional mode. Choosing his words carefully, Ethan smiled when she seemed to have sorted things through.

"Bree, your trust is the greatest gift you can ever give us, and I want you to know it is a gift we will always cherish above all others. Hearing you say you are worried you can't be enough is astonishing when, in fact, you are already everything we've ever dreamed of and more, but I am sure my words won't ever convince you."

Lifting his hand, he slowly trailed the backs of his fingers down the side of her face until he could push his hand through her soft curls and grasp her nape, he saw her eyes go wide and was thrilled to see them fill with desire.

"The only way for you to understand the power you hold as a submissive is to experience it both vicariously and personally. Have any of the subs you've spent time with mentioned sub-space to you?" Ethan knew by her expression they had and the ghost of a smile on her lips made him anxious to hear what her new friends had said.

"They mentioned it briefly, mostly they just fanned themselves while their eyes glazed over and said it was something I had to experience myself to fully understand. When I told them I'd read about the endorphin rush and how the flood of the happy chemicals in the brain... What? See, now you are giving me the same look they gave me."

JAMIE LEANED OVER and spoke close enough to her ear, she could feel his warm breath move over her skin like a lover's caress.

"Stop thinking like a physician, *Chère*. Sub-space is an experience we hope to give you very, very soon, but it is not something I think any two people experience in exactly the same way. I'm glad they didn't give you any preconceived expectations because that allows your first time to be oh so much more intense. God, I can hardly wait for the moment when that quick mind of yours lets go and you float into a state of bliss."

Bree felt as if his words were drawing her in like a moth to a flame. His voice was almost hypnotizing, and she wondered if it was possible to come just from listening to someone describe pleasure. She heard him chuckle and suddenly realized—much to her horror—she'd spoken her thoughts aloud.

"You are the most amazing woman I've ever met. There are so many fascinating layers that make you who you are, we'll spend the next sixty years discovering new things each day and still barely scratch the surface."

Jamie was so close she could feel his heat pulsing against her skin. The air between them was so electrically charged with sexual energy, it was practically crackling. What was it about these men that set them apart from all the others? She respected the other Doms she'd met since she'd arrived at ShadowDance, but none of them made her want to do whatever it took to please them. Kat's words came back to her, and Bree suddenly understood her friend's devastation when she felt she'd let her husbands down. The moment of self-realization stunned her.

Holy hellcats, I might end up getting the hang of this submission thing after all.

Chapter 30

ETHAN WATCHED THE emotions play out over Bree's face. Jesus, Joseph, and sweet Mother Mary, the woman captivated him in ways he'd never dreamed possible. She was submissive to the bone, and he'd bet his last nickel she'd just realized it on some soul-deep level. The look of epiphany had been unmistakable, and he was grateful she'd finally seen in herself what he and Creed had seen from that first day. Thinking back on that day and how it had changed his life, he vowed to buy Catherine Lamont a huge bouquet the next time she visited.

Catherine had sent Bree to them because she'd known of Bree's curiosity about Ds relationships. When he'd spoken with her after Bree was shot, she'd told him she'd known he and Jamie would be perfect to introduce the timid woman to the joys of submission. He'd assured Catherine that Bree was indeed absolutely perfect, and he'd be forever in her debt for sending her to ShadowDance. Ethan had an enormous amount of respect for the elder Lamonts, and while they had been wildly successful in every business venture they'd ever undertaken, it was their generosity that made them so special.

Ethan had grown up surrounded by people who were unimaginably wealthy, but he'd never met anyone as open with their checkbooks or their hearts as Daniel and Catherine Lamont. Their domestic violence shelters were not only much-needed havens for victims, but they also offered educational opportunities for the residents and their children. He didn't doubt for a moment Catherine Lamont was Daniel's sub, and he was grateful she was open enough about her personal relationship to mentor other women.

Catherine was a wonderful example of how intelligent women don't lose anything by being submissive, actually, the truth was the exact opposite. Extremely intelligent women tended to recognize the freedom submission afforded them and the joy of not being responsible for their own pleasure. Most of the women Ethan had known who were what he'd jokingly termed *super-subs* enjoyed being able to place the reins in someone else's hands. They often told him how much they relished knowing their only responsibility was to obey. They didn't get bogged down in all the usual questions and insecurities—*Am I doing this right? Should I do this or that now?*

Knowing he and Creed could give Bree that kind of freedom was satisfying indeed. They'd discussed taking their little beauty to The Club in the near future because gauging a sub's reactions to scenes was a great way to find out exactly what interested them in order to push their boundaries.

At other times, a sub either didn't realize something was a trigger, or they were too embarrassed to admit it, but their reaction to seeing a scene involving that element was a dead giveaway. Even when their words said one thing, their body's response always told the tale. It was a very rare person who could control their body language for more than a few minutes. Every good Dom was an expert at reading body language, it was just a part of the definition.

Looking up at Creed, he knew he and his friend were

thinking the same thing. Yes, their beautiful Bree was going to see some interesting things tonight, and he could hardly wait to discover the sweet secrets tucked away in the depths of her sexuality. Ethan leaned forward and kissed her. It wasn't a kiss of passion or possession, but a kiss intended to assure her they'd been listening, not only to the words she'd spoken but also to those she'd hadn't had the courage to say—yet.

Chapter 31

BREE WAS SO nervous during dinner, she'd barely been able to eat a bite despite both Ethan's and Jamie's glares. She'd almost jumped for joy when they told her they planned to take her to The ShadowDance Club tonight. As they'd explained more and more of what would be expected of her, she'd begun to doubt whether she was ready. They had assured her they would be with her every moment, and as long as she remembered to be respectful, no one would hold her up to any unreasonable expectations during her first visit.

Knowing Kat would be there with Zach had also gone a long way to ease her anxiety, well, at least until she'd remembered Kat's description of the stocks and paddling she'd gotten. Bree had been standing near Mitch at the time, and he'd chuckled before leaning over and assuring her Katarina had been sorely testing both Alex and Zach's patience that evening and her outburst at the bar had merely been the straw that broke the Dom's back, so to speak. When Bree had looked at him skeptically, he'd smiled and reminded her that he was an empath and that she "thought loud" which had made her giggle.

During dinner, her men had to remind her several times to keep her legs spread wide, so they had unimpeded access to all of her *sweet spots*. And they'd certainly taken full advantage of their access. Holy hell, if they'd been trying to distract her from her worries about what she'd encounter at The Club, it had certainly been effective even if it had gotten awfully close to mortifying a time or two.

She'd wondered if she would ever eat an entire dinner at the Lamonts' table without having an orgasm and had looked up to see Mitch Grayson snort in laughter. Knowing she had turned fourteen shades of red, she'd ducked her head and hoped he'd keep it to himself. *Yeah, right, like that is going to happen.*

When she'd finally gotten up the courage to look up again, Mitch was watching her with an amused expression. He mouthed "doubtful" before laughing out loud. Ethan and Jamie watched the interplay and promised her they would be expecting an explanation, causing her to flush yet again.

"Did we mention that Mitch has a new invention he has asked us to test this evening, *Chère?*" Jamie's saccharin-sweet words didn't match the dark intent she saw in his eyes. She knew a setup when she heard one. She was determined not to fall into the trap, so she decided to wait for him to elaborate. After all... there are questions, then there are rhetorical questions designed to set up someone with less worldly experience... *like me.* "It's a state-of-the-art sensor, it'll send data to various devices, including our phones."

Oh shit, this can't be good. I'm just betting it sends data. I'll bet it sends a whole encyclopedia of information I might not particularly be of a mind to share. Geez, I swear that Mitch is too smart for his own good. Crap, crap, crap don't think this stuff, he'll hear it all.

"What kind of data?" She had barely recognized her own voice, it had been soft, but even she could hear the curiosity laced through her tone.

"Why don't you go to the ladies' room. When you're finished meet us on the back deck, so we can explain all the wonderful little details of Master Mitch's newest gadget. Don't be long, *Chère*, or I *will* come and get you."

Bree found herself walking numbly away from the table. All their teasing words were having their desired effect, she was balanced right on the edge of anticipation and fear.

STEPPING OUT ONTO the deck a few minutes later, Bree was surprised to see several Doms but no other subs. When she started to take a step back, Ethan took her hand and pulled her close.

"Don't look so scared, little sub. Mitch wanted to explain the device to several of us at one time and he has done so. He has asked that you test his invention for several reasons I'll let him explain to you. If after hearing what he has to say, you don't want to try it, you just need to say no. There will not be any repercussions or consequences, do you understand?"

Bree must have a deer-in-the-headlights expression because most of the Doms surrounding her chuckled, and she heard Colt Matthews say, "I think you need to get on with the explanation, Grayson. Bree is looking a little pale, and it's been my experience that very bright women have imaginations that are much more creative than our reality." His words pulled her back to more solid footing, and Bree was very grateful.

Mitch stepped forward and opened his palm. Bree was surprised to see a relatively insignificant looking device that reminded her a lot like a small version of the bullet vibrators she'd seen in the specialty shops she and her roommates had visited in college. When she looked up at him in confusion, he laughed, then looked at Ethan and Jamie.

"I have known you two for a long time, and honest to God, I have no idea what you could have ever done to deserve her. She is an absolute delight." When he returned his attention to her, she saw his eyes soften. "You and Rissa are going to be wonderful friends. And just so you know, personally, I'm so glad you're here. Now, let me tell you why you are the perfect person to test drive this prototype."

Bree listened while Mitch explained how the device monitored the female body's autonomic responses to arousal. He'd skipped most of the technical stuff about how the data was sent to a mainframe to be analyzed and interpreted before being forwarded to the sub's Dominant partner. She'd listened intently until he finished.

"So basically, this is an internally placed lie detector?"

Mitch had been so surprised by her simple but dead-on analysis of everything he'd told her, that he was momentarily speechless. She heard the other men chuckle, then caught Alex Lamont's observation.

"Well, I'll be damned, I can't say that I have ever seen Grayson speechless. Congratulations, Bree. Well done, my mother will be convinced it's due to her influence." For a moment, she was so surprised Alex had actually made a joke, she was too stunned to react. When she looked at him, she saw the mirth in his expression, so she nodded her head once in acknowledgment of his roundabout compliment.

Jamie stepped forward, wrapped his arms around her

from the back, and pressed his hard length against her, immediately bringing her back to the topic at hand. Her body recognized its Master and had no trouble interpreting the unspoken message. It was his way of reminding her this was a scene of sorts and respect was the order of the day. Leaning down so his lips were close to her ear, he spoke words that were for her alone, but were heard by everyone assembled nearby.

"*Chère*, we are waiting for your answer about wearing the device. Because of your lack of previous experience with the things you are going to see during this first foray into a BDSM club, you are an ideal person to test Master Mitch's new toy. We'd like to slip it into you, right here, right now with all these Doms watching. Your compliance would please your Masters very much, but as always, the choice is yours. What is your answer?"

Bree knew every Dom standing on the large deck could read her body's instant response to Jamie's words without the benefit of the device because her knees had nearly folded out from under her. She wasn't sure she would have remained upright if it hadn't been for Jamie's arm banded around her shoulders.

JAMIE WAS CONVINCED Bree had been too distracted to realize the entire time he'd been talking to her, he'd been running his fingers through her wet folds. She hadn't been at all concerned with his hand snaking up under the front of her short dress. Bree was already fully on display and their evening had already started.

Every Dom around them was watching her reactions,

and Bree's slide into submission was truly something to behold. Her breathing had become so shallow, she was almost panting, and the smell of her arousal had sweetened the night air. He had enfolded her and watched in a nearby mirror as her eyelids slid down and her head tipped back onto his shoulder. Her softly whispered, "Yes" was all they needed.

Mitch reached over and tapped a few keys on his laptop, then handed the small bullet-shaped device to Jamie.

"Let Master Ethan help you spread your legs, *Chère*, then I'm going to use my fingers to slide this inside your sweet body. Every man near us is going to hear and see my fingers sliding through the slick petals of your pussy. They're going to know how wet you are for your Masters, and I want you to know that pleases us both very much. That's right, let Master Ethan open you up to accept this gift. Your body is ready, your clit is already seeking the attention of my fingers, isn't it, *Chère*?"

Her softly groaned affirmation was enough to send blood rushing into his already rock-hard cock. Jamie was thrilled she was so lost in the moment, she hadn't even realized Ethan had already placed the small device deeply inside her while Jamie continued to rub small circles around her clit. Excitement lit Mitch's eyes as the screen in front of him began filling with numbers and lines of text. Jamie smiled to himself when he felt his cell phone vibrate in his pocket, no doubt telling him what he already knew, that the sweet sub in his arms was a hair's breadth from orgasm.

God, she was incredible. Jamie would bet if you'd asked her earlier today if she was an exhibitionist, she'd have given you an emphatically negative response, but her sweet body was telling a different tale. Tightening his arm around her possessively, he simply said, "Come for me, *Chère.*"

Bree's entire body shuddered in his arms a split second before she screamed her release. Her cream washed over his fingers, and he felt her vaginal walls pulsing even though he had kept his fingers just outside her opening. He was grateful the other men had returned to the house by the time she had opened her eyes because he wasn't sure she was ready to face so many Doms when she would be feeling the most vulnerable. It was the rare submissive who didn't need a few minutes of recovery time after a public scene.

Ethan stepped forward and wrapped her in a warm soft blanket before lifting her into his arms and carrying her to a nearby glider. As Jamie moved with them, he made sure she saw him licking his fingers.

"You taste so sweet on my fingers, *Chère*. I don't want to waste any of this tasty gift." When she smiled faintly, he leaned closer and kissed her. "You did beautifully. Your soul sings with pleasure at our touch, and we'll spend the rest of our lives bringing you pleasure if you'll let us."

Jamie knew Bree was still floating and his words hadn't fully penetrated her consciousness yet. He'd simply hoped to plant the seed in her mind to smooth the way for the plans they'd made for the end of their evening.

"Let Ethan hold you for a few minutes while I check on something inside, then we'll head over to The Club with the others."

When he started to stand, she reached out and grasped his hand. She surprised him when she whispered her thanks for making her first exhibition scene so easy. He smiled and shook his head. It was going to take everything he and Ethan had—combined—to keep ahead of her lightning-quick mind. He'd been wrong to assume she was so lost in the haze of arousal that she hadn't understood exactly what he was doing. There wasn't anything about her that didn't tempt and astound him.

Chapter 32

JAMIE WALKED INTO Alex and Zach's office to find Mitch leaning over his laptop, typing furiously and beaming at the screen. When he finally looked up to see Jamie standing in front of him, Mitch smiled.

"She is amazing. I hope you and Jantz know how lucky you are."

Laughing and shaking his head at his friend, Jamie said, "We do. Where is your sweet wife? Does Tink know you are lusting after our woman?" Rissa had been nicknamed Tink, short for Tinkerbell when she'd first come to The Club as an aesthetician and massage therapist. She was tiny, flighty, and her beautiful red hair had also helped earn her the nickname. But it had been Rissa's wounded soul that had made her the unofficial "kid sister" of almost every Dom at The Club.

"She and Bry are already over at The Club. I'm joining them in a few minutes. We'll wait until she has a chance to speak with Bree for a few minutes, then Bryant will be taking her home. As much as we all miss playing at The Club, neither Bryant nor I are willing to share her lushly pregnant body with you perverted bastards."

Chuckling as he folded his computer Mitch added, "The device is working beautifully. The data stream is incredible. I hadn't even considered the potential uses with victims until Bree. Of course, we'd have to use more traditional monitoring methods, but it would still have great applications for learning more about what various stimuli trigger adverse responses."

Mitch must have noticed everyone in the room had gone silent and had that 'What the fuck is he talking about?' expression on their face, because he looked genuinely baffled before he rolled his eyes and said, "Ignorant bunch of soldier boys. Christ, what did I ever do to deserve this?"

Alex Lamont looked at him and rolled his eyes. "The list is nearly endless." Everyone in the room laughed and Mitch just shook his head.

"I'll leave this laptop behind the bar, so it processes and sends you the texts this evening. I'll be monitoring things from the Crow's Nest, I have first shift tonight. The wireless isn't powerful enough to work at any great distance yet, but I'll figure that part out before long." Mitch turned to leave the room, but Jamie stopped him.

"Grayson, I—well, I just wanted to say thanks. Your help is going to go a long way to help us keep Bree in a good place tonight. We're anxious for her to experience everything our lifestyle has to offer, but it's nice to know we've got this safety net." Mitch just nodded once before heading once again toward the door.

Jamie had always admired Mitch's techno-savvy and envied empathic gifts. He knew the man's skills had been huge assets to several SEAL teams. Their stories were legendary, and even though they were likely greatly exaggerated, the essence was damned impressive. Jamie saw Mitch stop at the door, then the other man turned back. Mitch stood studied him for so long, Jamie finally raised an eyebrow in question. Sighing heavily, Mitch cocked head toward the deck.

"I really should keep my mouth shut, but I know you are worried, and I'd rather your woman has your full attention tonight. And as great as my little invention is, it can't tell you everything." Mitch had paused for so long, Jamie started to get nervous. He finally took a deep breath and continued, "She wants to stay, but she wants to know for sure that you want her. Remarkably, that incredible woman is insecure. She loves her new friends and wants to practice medicine again—*here*—almost as much as she wants you two. But she is also worried about her dad and whether or not he'd ever fit in here in Climax." Glancing in Alex's direction, Mitch grinned, "Just FYI, her dad is apparently a hell of a carpenter and handyman as well as a communications specialist. Go figure."

Alex was leaning back in his chair with his feet propped up on his ornate desk and merely nodded, evidently giving Mitch permission to share the next piece of information before Grayson added, "Alex doesn't see a problem with helping him out once the feds are finished with him."

Jamie was relieved at least one of Bree's worries was going to be easily set aside, and if his friends had made these plans, it was likely the older man would be released soon rather than later.

"Word is her medical license is a done deal and she knows it," Mitch continued. "Catherine called her about an hour ago. So, I'd say she's letting it all ride until she is convinced she's *enough* for you and Jantz." Mitch seemed to sigh with relief he'd gotten it all off his chest, but he turned back one last time before walking through the door. "Bree Hart is golden, don't fuck this up." Everyone in the room understood the significance of what Mitch had just said. *Golden* was a team term for pure, honest, and good, through and through. While Jamie appreciated the validation, he'd already known it.

Now all he and Jantz had to do was convince Bree she was everything they'd always hoped and dreamed for and more…

Chapter 33

JAMIE AND ETHAN had discussed Bree's first visit to The Club in excruciating detail, including requesting assistance from several other Doms along with their very willing subs. After working with Bree on both her hard and soft limits, they'd been able to set up various scenes for her to observe. Some of the scenes they fully expected would totally turn her on while a couple of others they were guessing she wouldn't be as interested in.

They'd read and reread the detailed reports of her captivity, so they had purposely not included any equipment they felt might serve as a reminder of that time in her life. Bree was a survivor, but she was also still healing, so avoiding anything that might trigger a PTSD episode was a priority.

Everyone involved in this evening's activities, including each of the dungeon monitors had been thoroughly briefed. Nothing was being left to chance—Bree was just too precious to put at risk.

They had decided Ethan would take the lead as Bree's escort while Jamie would be nearby, monitoring the incoming texts and troubleshooting. When Alex Lamont reviewed the plan without making a single adjustment, Jamie had been convinced they'd overplanned themselves into oblivion. Their boss was well known as being meticulous to a fault, so if he hadn't wanted to make any changes, everyone agreed they'd moved deep into the "overkill" zone.

They gave Bree a few minutes to return to her suite and freshen up, but it was almost time to meet her at the bottom of the front stairs. Jamie made sure he was in place because he wanted to see her as she descended the beautifully curved staircase.

The stairs were ornately carved mahogany and had always reminded Jamie of Scarlett's home in *Gone with the Wind*. He looked up just as Bree started down the stairs, and it was as if the whole world had suddenly gone into slow motion. The low light from the wall sconces sent golden rays out to dance over her lightly tanned skin. Her hair was the stuff of every man's fantasies, and her gray eyes were filled with the perfect mix of apprehension and curiosity.

He held out his hand and helped her down the last step before saying, "You are a vision, *Chère*. Are you ready to go?" She simply smiled sweetly and nodded, so he led her out of the house. As they walked the short distance along the edge of the gardens making their way to The Club, Jamie stopped and lifted Bree up onto one of the rock ledges, so he could look directly into his tiny sub's beautiful eyes. "I want to take just a minute before we enter The Club to remind you of four things.

"First, during this first trip, we'll expect you to have a lot of questions, and we encourage you to ask everyone. Be sure you ask Ethan's permission before speaking to anyone other than Ethan or me. The second is, make sure you speak very quietly while observing a scene. It is considered very rude to distract the participants or your fellow observers. Third, even though Ethan will be your principle host for this evening, remember I will never be far away."

What he hadn't explained was he would be closely monitoring the data feeds and incoming texts. His military training and background included emergency response medical information which gave him a good working knowledge of the body's symptoms and signals of an emotional break, so he would be using the data from Grayson's prototype to watch for more than just sexual responses.

Ethan had been the logical choice to take the lead tonight because being a Dom was imprinted on the man's DNA. He came from a long line of Dominants. His father had literally started training him from the time he'd been a small child. Whereas Jamie had been raised by his *grand-mère*, so his introduction to the lifestyle had come much later.

Jamie enjoyed being dominant in the bedroom but didn't have any problem enjoying romantic interludes of straight vanilla lovemaking. Ethan, on the other hand, would be left completely unsatisfied by any vanilla encounter. As a true submissive, Bree would also suffer because her deep desire to please her Dom would prevent her from enjoying any scene that left him unfulfilled.

Placing his hand on the sides of her heart-shaped face, Jamie lightly stroked her cheeks with his thumbs, ensuring her focus was entirely on the last thing he wanted her to remember. He would never forget how grateful he was to the Universe for giving him this second chance with her. Everything about her enchanted him. Even now, as anxious and as apprehensive as she was feeling about this plunge into the deep end of the BDSM pool, she was totally "in the moment" with him. Jamie took a deep breath.

"The fourth and by far the most important thing you

need to remember is that I love you. Keep that written in your heart, so you'll always know right where to find me." When her eyes filled with unshed tears, he worried that he'd gone too far, but her words quickly washed away his doubt.

"I love you, too, probably more than I should because my life really is still a bit of a mess. I know I'm not fully recovered, and I'm not even sure I ever will be, but I know that I love you and Ethan both. I'm so grateful to Catherine for sending me here."

Jamie felt as if his heart had doubled in size, and he spent long seconds just floating in the warm glow of the love he saw written so clearly in her expression. Knowing he'd given Ethan plenty of time to see to the last-minute details, he finally found his words. He leaned close, so his quietly spoken words would move against her ear like a warm caress over her delicate ear.

"Let's go, *Chère*. Master Ethan and a whole new world await you."

Chapter 34

ETHAN WATCHED AS Jamie led their lovely woman toward The Club's garden entrance. The dress she was wearing was just barely on this side of transparent, and the backlighting of the garden's fairy lights was highlighting her curves. She was still too slender, but Selita's wonderful cooking coupled with the self-defense training she'd been practicing with the other women, they were starting to see shades of the woman she had been before her kidnapping. Ethan still had to tamp down his rage every time he thought about how her life had been thrown so tragically off course simply because she'd had the misfortune of being born to parents who weren't smart enough to protect their greatest treasure.

He could see her silky blonde cloud of curls cascading around her shoulders before falling down her bare back in a waterfall of varying shades of yellows and golds. As she got closer, he could see her eyes were shining with apprehension laced with anticipation—*Perfect*.

When he held out his hand, Jamie placed the small hand he'd been holding in Ethan's larger one. It was a small but symbolic transfer of power and watching as her eyes dilated with arousal, Ethan knew the significance hadn't been lost on her.

"Welcome to The ShadowDance Club, my love. Both

Master Jamie and I are thrilled you are here. We have been looking forward to this evening for a long time. More importantly, we have been waiting *for you* forever." He paused as much to let his own thoughts catch up with his emotions as he did to let his words settle over her. He was pleased to see a bit of the tension drain from her posture.

"I know Master Jamie reviewed some of the rules, but I want to add a couple of things as well." Reaching to the cuffs clipped to the back of his belt, he unhooked them, so she could see the soft leather was lined, so they wouldn't chafe her delicate skin. "Give me your wrists, Love." Watching her eyes go wide as her body trembled in excitement was the sexiest thing he'd ever seen. Her breathing hitched, but she placed her wrists in his open palm without hesitation. "Such a good girl, thank you for your trust."

He used his thumbs to rub small circles over her pulse points after he'd buckled the cuffs and checked they weren't tight enough to cause any discomfort or cut off her circulation.

"These will tell anyone who sees them you belong to us. They are an added layer of protection. I don't ever plan to be more than a breath away from you, but this is a way to make sure no Dom approaches you directly. You will see there are many ways leather and jewels can be used by Doms to mark their subs. Feel free to look for those, so you will have some ideas for your own when that time comes." When he saw her glance warily at her wrists, he knew exactly where her mind had gone.

"No, Love, these cuffs have never been on any other sub. We would never degrade you with something that had been used on another woman. Everything that touches your sweet body will have been purchased specifically with you in mind." When he saw a hint of doubt, he stepped closer, crowding into her personal space before letting some of his usual steel back into his voice.

"Think of it this way. We are your Doms and that means your body is ours to care for and use as we see fit. Each and every decision we make will be with your best interests in mind. Don't ever doubt that we will *always* take very good care of what belongs to us."

Ethan continued to watch her as her fingers absently traced over the soft leather cuffs. His heart nearly burst when she looked up at him through her sun-kissed lashes and smiled sweetly.

"Thank you for the beautiful gift, Sirs."

Tucking her small hand into his elbow, he nodded to Jamie before turning and walking Bree into what he hoped was going to be one of the most wonderful nights of their lives. He was keenly aware that this was a make-or-break moment. There was so much riding on their success introducing Bree to their lifestyle, he'd lain awake last night scrutinizing every detail of their elaborate plan. While he loved Bree deeply, he wasn't sure he'd ever feel completely fulfilled in a permanent relationship with her unless she recognized his need for dominance and freely gave him her submission. Ethan knew Jamie was behind them and had seen him slip his phone out and glance at it, and the smile that had twitched at the corner of his friend's mouth had told him what he needed to know… It was show time.

Chapter 35

BREE HAD BARELY had time to catch her breath after her experience on the back deck and her body was fully on board with whatever was planned for this evening, but her mind was still trying to process everything. If you had asked her a few weeks ago if she was an exhibitionist, she would have given you an unequivocal *No!*

When she'd been "introduced" to Mitch Grayson's newest invention, knowing there were other Doms watching had been a major turn-on. Jamie had brought her to an orgasm that had sent her spiraling into orgasmic oblivion and nearly turned her bones to mush.

I still think Jamie could talk me into an orgasm using nothing more than that sex-in-the-form-of-sound voice of his.

Ethan and Jamie had given her way too few minutes to get herself together for "Round 2" as Kat had labeled it. Thank God Kat's suite was only a few steps from the one Bree was using and her new friend had helped her freshen up because she wasn't sure she could have remained focused enough on her own.

You gotta love those lovely little endorphins.

When Bree had stood, staring blankly in the mirror, she'd quickly learned Katarina Lamont could be a force of nature. The tiny woman had kept Bree moving and made sure all her "bits," as Kat had called them, were covered;

well, as covered as anything could be in a dress made of fabric so thin, you could probably read through it. Kat had brushed her hair and supervised her make-up touch-ups before sending her on her way.

Walking down the front stairs into Jamie's waiting arms had made her feel like Cinderella heading to the ball. Well, until she realized her Prince Charming was one of two and the ball was a kinky sex club. It had taken all of her willpower to not giggle at her own musings.

Standing in the gardens listening to Jamie's last-minute coaching and reminders had given her a chance to steel herself for what was to come. His sweet confession of love had wrapped itself securely around her heart and made everything inside her warm for the first time since before her kidnapping. She knew the future she'd always dreamed of was finally firmly within her reach, and the significance of her acceptance of their lifestyle was not lost on her.

Walking in the garden entrance to The Club, the first thing she noticed was the heavy beat of the music. Kat had explained most kink clubs played very hard driving music, but The ShadowDance Club liked to keep things more casual, so they played a variety of music. Bree had never really gotten into the whole music fan thing like most young women. Most of the remote locations they'd lived in, she'd had such limited access, valuable computer time had always been reserved for studying.

Whatever was playing over the overhead speakers now seemed to have a nice Caribbean beat, and she remembered they'd all sung along to this song during their recent margarita party. She smiled, knowing Kat had kept her promise to make sure she felt at home the minute she walked in the door. Bree had learned Katarina Lamont was a huge Kenny Chesney fan, so the music was Kat's way of saying, "Welcome."

Entering the Main Lounge, they made their way over to the bar where Ethan introduced her to Cort Douglas who he'd explained was The Club's bartender, and Sally Reed. It had been obvious to Bree the two were a couple and Ethan explained that until recently, Cort had also headed up The Club's training program for submissives. After he and Sally had finally gotten together, he resigned from that position.

Sally requested permission to address Bree directly, and both Cort and Ethan had agreed, but Bree was still a bit surprised when the gorgeous young woman wrapped her in a big hug.

"We are so glad you are here. Those two men of yours have been looking for their third for a long while, and it's obvious to everyone who sees the three of you, you're the one. I sure do hope you stick around, I have a little girl, and I'd like to take her to a doctor who didn't scare the bejeebus out of her." Sally leaned in and gave her another quick hug before adding, "Now, I need to get moving, but if you have any questions, please don't hesitate to ask. I promise you can't ask anything that will embarrass me." With those words, Sally moved away, and Bree was lost in her own thoughts for a minute before she felt Ethan move in behind her.

When he wrapped his arms around her and cupped her breast through her dress, she recognized it as the power shift she was sure he had intended it to be.

"It's time for us to move on, Love." He pushed her hair to the side and leaned down, so his words were spoken directly into her ear. "Do you see how the other subs are dressed? Note, some of them are wearing nothing but the adornments their Masters have chosen. They are not hiding their bodies because it pleases their Masters to show off what belongs to them. Would you enjoy being naked if it pleased your Masters, Love?"

Bree felt her breathing catch and she knew her pulse had quickened, but it was the rush of moisture from her pussy that had really given her away. Ethan pulled up the hem of her dress and ran his fingers through her folds and chuckled behind her. "I think that idea excites you, Love. Good to know. That is something we can explore, but not tonight."

Bree had been so focused on the warm brush of his breath on her skin and the feel of his fingers sliding over her rapidly swelling labia, she hadn't even realized he had exposed her bare pussy to anyone who had been looking.

Holy hell, I may be an exhibitionist after all.

When he turned her toward what he called "The Play Room," she saw it was actually the other side of the lounge area. As they walked closer, the space reminded her of a movie set she'd seen once years ago when she and her parents had vacationed in London. She was surprised to see how varied the scene areas were, and she shuddered involuntarily at the realizations that brought forth.

Ethan stopped and turned her, so she faced him. "Are you cold, Love? Or have you seen something that caused that shudder?"

Damn, he isn't going to miss a thing. She wanted him to know she was still *on board*, so she met his gaze before speaking.

"No, Sir, I'm not cold. I just realized the scope of this lifestyle is much broader than I'd realized. This whole... well, this area kind of reminds me of a movie set, and I just hadn't realized how much there was... it's overwhelming, but it's also very exciting."

His smile had been enough to melt her heart. The relief flashing in his eyes was easy to see. "You have no idea how happy I am to hear those words, Love." Ethan turned her back, so she was once again facing the scene area and leaned down and pressed a kiss to the sensitive spot where her shoulder sloped up into her neck. "Let's go explore, shall we?"

Bree felt a rush of excitement race through her entire body, and for the first time since he and Jamie had started talking to her about their plans for this evening, she felt everything really could work out fine. As the tension began draining from her body, she hurried to keep up with the long length of his stride.

As they approached the first small stage, Ethan reminded her, "Remember to be completely honest in your answers to my questions, Love. Your honesty is paramount." When she looked up at him, he kissed her on the forehead and added, "That includes being honest with yourself, sweet Bree, never forget that."

Taking in the first scene, Bree saw a lushly curved woman strapped to a padded leather table. Soft music played nearby, and Bree noticed the woman's eyes were covered by what looked like a silk scarf. Even though Bree couldn't hear what the leather-clad man was saying to her, she could hear the woman's soft moans as her Dom brushed a feather over her skin.

His movements we fluid and deliberately placed, reminding Bree of a Renaissance artist painting his greatest masterpiece. Bree smiled at her own observation because, in an odd sort of way, it was very fitting. She knew Ethan had seen her smile when he leaned close.

"Tell me what that thought was, Love." After she explained, he'd nodded his head, smiling in agreement.

Whispering close to her ear, he prompted, "Tell me what you see and feel when you watch this scene."

She watched for a few more minutes, taking time to really consider what she was feeling and without taking her eyes off the scene, she answered.

"I'm not sure I'd like being tickled with a feather, I'm terribly ticklish and it doesn't really turn me on if you know what I mean. But I can see how intense it would be to have your Dom totally focused on igniting pleasure all over your body while you were unable to move. I really do believe Master Jamie could talk me right over the edge of orgasm because he has a hypnotic voice. He uses it to paint a picture in my mind, and that is very powerful." When she finally looked up, she saw him smiling at her.

"Your observations and honesty please me very much, Love." She suddenly realized he was rubbing small circles lightly over the small of her back, and it was like sinking into a tub of warm pleasure. "But just so you know, you are probably wrong about the tickling because she is feeling many different sensations. I'd be willing to wager she wouldn't describe any of them as tickling."

Laughing quietly, he reached up and used the lightest of touches to brush her hair over her shoulder, and she felt the shudder start at her core and work its way to the surface. "Now, Love, would you describe that as *tickling* or something entirely different?"

She gasped and was surprised at how airy her voice sounded when she was finally able to squeak out, "Oh my. I understand... Sir. That's really amazing." As he moved her toward the next scene, her knees felt weak, and she was grateful when they found a seat on one of the front sofas directly in front of the second small stage.

Chapter 36

ETHAN WAS THRILLED with Bree's willingness to be completely open about her physical and emotional responses to the first scene. Judging by Creed's quick hand signals, her body was responding exactly as they hoped it would. He seated her on his lap and pulled her back against his chest, so she would be completely open to his touch. The position also let him closely monitor her responses.

This was the first scene where she might easily misinterpret what was happening unless she was watching closely. Just as he had pulled her against him, he felt her whole-body tense, and squeezed her tight.

"Tell me what you see... look closely, Love." It was several seconds before she answered, and Ethan had started to worry until he'd seen Creed's quick signal that they were still good to go.

"I see a large square frame that looks as though it might turn like a lazy Susan or pivot from the center to lie flat like a table. The woman is tethered to the inside of the frame at her ankles and wrists, so she is completely open to her two masters. There is also a thick leather belt around her waist for added support. There are clamps on her nipples, and they are so dark and peaked so tightly, I know she must be able to feel each beat of her heart." He was fascinated with her observations, but he wanted to fill in a few of the blanks.

"First of all, I want you to notice you haven't mentioned that both of the subs have been completely naked, and that pleases me because it shows an open-mindedness that is rare for anyone's first visit to a BDSM club. Also, take a closer look at the cuffs. The lining is very soft; watch as the Doms check the fit frequently to make sure her circulation isn't cut off and her fingers are still pink and warm. If her fingers start tingling, she'll use her safe word or 'yellow' to let them know there's a problem. I want to remind you the most severe punishment any sub at The ShadowDance Club ever receives is for his or her failure to look out for their personal safety—in or out of a scene. Failing to use your safe word is an offense that is *always* dealt with publicly and harshly—remember that, Love."

When she nodded her understanding and murmured, "Yes, Sir," he continued his narration of the scene.

"The Doms you see here are doing a demonstration. They are extremely skilled with the instruments they are using, and I'm happy they agreed to do this scene." He chuckled and said, "There was a mad scramble of volunteers among the uncollared subs to participate in this scene. These Dominants often do public scenes, thus the rapidly growing crowd around us." He bit down lightly on her earlobe, then sucked it into his mouth, soothing the sting, before adding, "They agreed to do this for you, Love, so let's show them how much you appreciate their efforts by sitting as you are required to at dinner and give them your complete attention."

When Bree had spread her legs wide apart, he gently tugged her dress up, so her bare pussy was open to his touch and clearly visible to anyone who wanted to look. Her exposure hadn't escaped the attention of either of the

Doms performing on the small stage. They both nodded their approval to Ethan, and he felt her cheek heat against his own and knew she was blushing.

"Flogging sensitizes the skin by bringing the blood to the surface. It can be used as a prelude or warm-up to something more intense or can be the entire purpose of the scene. A Dom skilled with a flogger can bring a sub to a screaming orgasm very quickly." She listened to Ethan's explanation and appeared to appreciate that he'd allowed her to simply watch. She noticed that the sub seemed to be kind of *disconnected*, and Ethan picked up her concern.

"Notice how she seems to be floating in her mind? She's entering sub-space, that wonderful endorphin-fueled happy place that is the goal of every scene."

It was just a few minutes until the sub was screaming as she came in huge shuddering waves of obvious pleasure. When she finally sagged in exhaustion, Bree watched with apparent relief when both Doms worked quickly to release the restraints. She followed the movements of the tall blond Dom as he wrapped the woman in a plush blanket, then carried her to a chair at the back of the scene area. Bree watched him speaking quietly to the woman several minutes after the people around them had filtered away.

When she refocused her attention, she finally noticed Ethan had moved her legs back together and lowered her dress. The Native American Dom knelt in front of her and was looking at her with a soft smile playing over his face.

"Hello, Bree. Welcome to ShadowDance, my name is Cash Red Cloud or Master Cash while we are here. I've heard a lot about you from your Masters, and I'm very pleased to meet you." Bree noticed what seemed to be a silent exchange between the two men before he continued speaking to her.

"I wanted to tell you that I was there the day you were rescued, and I can't begin to tell you how much of an inspiration you are to those of us who saw how you had been treated." She hadn't even realized she was crying until he reached up and wiped away her tears. "Please don't cry, *yazhi*. I just wanted you to know you never need fear the men who gave you these small badges of courage." As he spoke the words, he drew his fingers along one of the faint scars on her shoulder. "I promise you, none of them will ever hurt another woman."

Before she realized what she was doing, she leaned forward, kissed him softly on the cheek, and whispered, "Thank you… for coming to my rescue and for taking their cruel asses out."

Chapter 37

ETHAN HAD BEEN completely stunned by her words, and the look on Cash's face had been priceless. Cash Red Cloud was and always had been a true warrior in every sense of the word. His "run to the roar" approach to life had been the envy of every new recruit who had joined the teams. Watching as the man kneeling in front of Bree leaned his head back and howled in laughter had been wonderful.

Before Cash and Drake had returned to ShadowDance, Alex and Zach had told the team the most recent mission in South America had been successful, but extremely difficult. They hadn't been able to save a child who had stumbled into the crossfire, and both men had been shaken by the loss. As a result, they would both be getting some serious downtime in an effort to get them back on an even keel.

When Bree turned and touched his cheek, Ethan returned his focus to her.

"Master Ethan, I'm sorry for speaking to Master Cash without permission. I was so touched by what he'd said, I forgot I was supposed to ask."

Ethan was so surprised by her words he actually stuttered his response. "Oh—B–Bree, your response was completely natural and came directly from your heart. We won't ever punish you for expressing kindness or heartfelt gratitude." He stroked her hair and then hugged her close.

"Can I ask Master Cash a question please?" Her words were spoken softly and with such sincerity, there was no way he could deny her request.

"Of course. And thank you for remembering to ask, Love. You please me very much." Ethan watched as she turned to Cash and smiled.

"Master Cash, what does *yazhi* mean?"

Ethan watched as Cash smiled and raised his finger to lightly touch the very tip of Bree's nose in a clearly affectionate gesture.

"*Yazhi* was what my grandmother always called my younger sister, it's Navajo for 'little one.' You are beautiful, and your Masters are very lucky men indeed. I hope someday the Universe sends me a woman as brave as you." He smiled and winked before adding, "And beautiful would be a nice bonus as well." *From your lips to God's ears, my new friend.*

Ethan set Bree on her feet and stood to shake hands with Cash before the man moved back to help clean the scene area and pack up his duffel. Ethan turned back to Bree just as Creed joined them. Together they led Bree to one of the small private rooms, and he was pleased to see Jamie had taken time to light the candles and turn down the bed. Before they made love to her, they had to make sure she understood the commitment they were asking for.

He smiled when she turned in a circle, taking in the luxurious room. The Club offered a variety of "themed rooms" for private play, and this was the favorite of couples seeking a romantic setting for a scene, collaring ceremonies, or other special occasions.

"It's beautiful, and the candlelight is spectacular. Thank

you for making this night so memorable. I learned a lot about myself, and that many of my fears weren't based on fact."

Ethan stood back and watched as Jamie pulled Bree into his embrace, simply holding her for long minutes, whispering against her ear, telling her how pleased they were with her. He told her how wonderfully she had responded to everything they had shown her.

He also reminded her there certainly were more extreme methods of play, but neither he nor Ethan had ever been into anything more than she'd already seen or heard about from the other women. Jamie also told her how grateful he was for the kindness she'd shown Cash.

"Your kind spirit set a dear friend of ours back on a track tonight. That simple act from your heart will help heal his, *Chère*. Every member of our team will be indebted to you for that. You will never know what your actions and words meant to him. I haven't heard him laugh like that in a very long time, and it was awfully nice to see the old Cash again even if it was just a first glimpse."

When Jamie stepped back, Ethan moved to his side and they both stood facing Bree. Ethan watched as her eyes flashed with apprehension for just a second before she saw their smiles.

"Bree, you are everything Jamie and I have ever dreamed of finding in a woman. I know you are the one my sweet *grand-mère* has been assuring me was coming my way for a long time. She promised my soul would recognize the woman immediately, and she was right."

Jamie took her left hand in his as Ethan opened the small velvet box he'd carried in his pocket all evening. He took the ring from its nesting place and held it at the end of her ring finger.

"Bree, please do us the great honor of becoming our wife. We promise there will never be a day when you don't know how much we love and cherish you. We will support you in any way we can, personally, professionally, spiritually, and financially. You will never want for anything we can provide for you." Jamie slid the ring halfway onto her tiny finger and looked into the misty gray depths of her eyes.

"I fell in love with you the first time I looked into your eyes. There won't ever be a moment I won't be thanking God for bringing you back into my life. Will you marry us?"

Bree looked at both of them and Jamie saw her acceptance before she even spoke.

"I love you both so much. There were so many times before I was kidnapped, while I was chained to that filthy floor before you rescued me, and during my long recovery process that I prayed for a chance to love and be loved. Every night after you carried me out of hell, I dreamt of you. When my request to contact you was denied, I felt like I'd lost you forever. I can scarcely believe I've been given this second chance and want very much to be your wife."

Jamie slid the ring all the way down her finger and said, "The details are the easy part and I assure you, your new friends are going to be very happy to help plan the wedding of your dreams, but first, we have a surprise for you. We'll be leaving first thing tomorrow to travel to Houston, so you can meet Ethan's family, then we'll visit mine." Leaning down to kiss the ring that now adorned her slender finger he smiled.

"You'll get to float down that bayou in the pirogue, *Chère*. I want you to understand the simple joys of life and the peace you will always be able to find in our loving care.

We want to spend the rest of our lives showing you all the reasons you made the right decision when you agreed to join your life to ours. But first—Master Ethan, what do you think? I think our sweet sub has been an exceptionally good girl this evening and do believe she has earned a reward."

Ethan had been grateful Jamie had taken the lead because it had given him a chance to get a handle on the emotions threatening to swamp him. Looking down at their ring on her finger was the most satisfying thing he'd ever seen.

"I agree, but right now, I think I'd really like to get a look at the beautiful body she has just entrusted to our loving care." He glanced over at Jamie and knew he was on board by his sly smile. Looking back at Bree, he uttered the one-word command he looked forward to repeating again and again.

"Strip."

Books by Avery Gale

The ShadowDance Club
Katarina's Return – Book One
Jenna's Submission – Book Two
Rissa's Recovery – Book Three
Trace & Tori – Book Four
Reborn as Bree – Book Five
Red Clouds Dancing – Book Six
Perfect Picture – Book Seven

Club Isola
Capturing Callie – Book One
Healing Holly – Book Two
Claiming Abby – Book Three

Masters of the Prairie Winds Club
Out of the Storm
Saving Grace
Jen's Journey
Bound Treasure
Punishing for Pleasure
Accidental Trifecta
Missionary Position
Another Second Chance
Star-Crossed Miracles
Dusted Star
Lilly's Choice

The Wolf Pack Series
Mated – Book One
Fated Magic – Book Two
Tempted by Darkness – Book Three

The Knights of the Boardroom
Book One
Book Two
Book Three

The Morgan Brothers of Montana
Coral Hearts – Book One
Dancing with Deception – Book Two
Caged Songbird – Book Three
Game On – Book Four
Well Bred – Book Five

Mountain Mastery
Well Written
Savannah's Sentinel
Sheltering Reagan

Enchanted Holidays
The Christmas Painting

I would love to hear from you!

Website:
www.averygale.com

Facebook:
facebook.com/avery.gale.3

Twitter:
@avery_gale

Made in the USA
Middletown, DE
13 May 2019